THE WATCH

THE WATCH

BIBI BERKI was born to Hungarian parents in Cambridge, spent her childhood in Hull, and then settled in London. She trained as a news reporter and has worked for the BBC as well as regional and national titles. She writes fiction and non-fiction and co-runs a production company which specialises in audio dramas. She is married with two children.

THE WATCH

BIBI BERKI

SALT

CROMER

PUBLISHED BY SALT PUBLISHING 2021

2 4 6 8 10 9 7 5 3 1

First published in Great Britain in 2021 by
Salt Publishing Ltd
12 Norwich Road, Cromer, Norfolk N R27 0A X United Kingdom

www.saltpublishing.com

Salt Publishing Limited Reg. No. 5293401

A CIP catalogue record for this book is available from the British Library

I S B N 978 1 78463 237 3 (Paperback edition)
I S B N 978 1 78463 238 0 (Electronic edition)

Typeset in Neacademia by Salt Publishing

Printed and bound in Great Britain by Clays Ltd, Elcograf S.p.A

To Hrothi

PART ONE

1

THAT EVENING, I had gone for a run.

Even at seven-thirty, the air was still thick with heat and my legs dragged and my head ached within the first kilometre. The tourists were out, loitering on the narrow pavements, and having to sidestep them made me all the more irritable. And so I returned earlier than I'd intended and went back to the college gates, annoyed by my lassitude, and by all the other people who lingered and looked, taking things slowly, aimless, disengaged.

At the college gate I was told there was a message waiting for me in my pigeon-hole.

I would have missed it had I not been told about it.

I would have gone back to my room and showered and probably walked to the river to watch the sun go down and that would have been that.

No story to tell.

But I went to the pigeon-holes and found the single folded piece of paper and opened it there and then and read it. It was addressed to me by name and signed by Dr Erin Waghorn and she was asking me to come up to her college rooms at once.

I knew her name, though I'd never been taught by her. She was a philosopher and lived alone in an apartment in Old Court and, because she had no family, had been appointed as the pastoral tutor for undergraduates. I can't imagine it was a job that any academic relished, particularly the cut-off kind that populated the teaching staff in the college back then. I had seen Dr Waghorn occasionally attempting to chat with students on what I assumed were personal and pressing issues and she'd seemed caught, to me, trapped by things she neither delighted in nor understood. She bent down and proffered an ear in symbolic sympathy but her eyes had been fixed on the clock, or the shadowed staircase that led to her rooms. She was very tall and very slim and had the look of a starved hawk.

I wondered for a moment if I should go and change out of my damp shorts and T-shirt, but I wanted to get this over with first. I had a Coke in my fridge and I told myself that it would taste even better if there was no longer an appointment hanging over me.

The tapering staircase that led to her rooms was dark and instantly cold. I took the steps quickly, still with my heart set on the Coke, and stood outside her door and waited – I'm not sure what for. The landing was empty except for her name on a sign on the stone wall and a bucket and a mop a little further away, leaning against the wooden panelling and left ready, presumably, for the morning. The cleaners were everywhere, now that it was the end of the year, wiping the last term clean off the record.

Dr Waghorn opened the door and almost immediately turned her back on me, stalked over to a sofa, sat on it and waited. I hovered a moment before closing her door and taking a few steps into her living room. She was in a sleeveless black linen dress and the skin on her bare shoulders looked as though it were packed underneath with stones.

She looked up at me from her sofa and frowned.

"I was relieved," she said. "When I realised it was you."

I came a little closer and sat on the arm of a worn yellow

armchair. (I would have sat *in* it, but it already contained books and journals and anyway I wasn't going to join her on the sofa. She didn't want that either. You could tell.)

All I could do was frown straight back at her.

Dr Waghorn's rooms were sombre but not entirely unwelcoming. There was a reddish Persian rug between us and the panelled walls were hung with old political etchings. I could smell that she'd recently cooked something with red wine in it.

"I need someone to help me and I was glad to find you were hadn't gone home yet. Not many people around any more. Have you been doing some sort of exercise, by the way? In this heat?"

She was affronted and she pulled the neck of her dress away from her collar bones to demonstrate how uncomfortable it was simply to exist this oppressive evening.

I ought to point out that Dr Waghorn couldn't have been more than about 55 at that time, but as I was only 19, and had no grasp of middle life, I couldn't imagine why heat would be so much of an issue.

"I'm in the hockey First Eleven," I told her. "We usually train on a Tuesday night. I didn't want to miss out."

"Miss out?" she asked, genuinely puzzled.

"Didn't want to – I just like being active."

She smiled then but not at me. I knew she was amused by the bizarre idea of pointless exertion.

"Anyway," she said and stopped dead.

I thought of my Coke and shifted on the arm of the chair.

Hard to tell, now, which one of us resented the other more that stifling evening. I was still too young to be comfortable in the company of older, far more intelligent people. I felt I was being tested and that any failure in my character would simply confirm my fraudulent presence in such a prestigious place. It was a sickeningly regular occurrence in my psyche in those days, the sense of being found out and ridiculed. She was just fed up with all of us.

"I haven't taught you yet, have I?"

"Not yet," I replied. "I'm switching from economics to SPS."

"Ah. One of those."

I shook my head, as if to say: *no, not one of those. I'm different. You'll like me.*

"Then we'll cross swords later," she said. "In the Marx module. It's always a little bloody. Always a little bit of an exercise in disillusionment, I'm afraid."

Was I meant to say something clever? I formed a sentence, gathered together vocabulary, constructed my idea. Quickly, quickly.

But she cut through it. Moved on.

"So," she said and lightly punched a red silk cushion, transferring her irritation. "This is the thing. I have to go to an event this evening. Which means I need to turn to someone for help and . . ."

I waited.

". . . and, as I've said, I'm extremely relieved to find that you're the closest person to hand. I know - having spoken about you with colleagues - that you're considered very responsible and - I think I'm right in this - a *caring* sort of person. You run some kind of group for the friendless, is that it?"

I was taken aback.

"I'm just on the social committee, that's all. We get people in to give talks." I had no idea where this *friendless* came in.

6

Did they laugh about us, I wondered?

"Oh, is that it? Well, it all suggests a community spirit, am I right?"

I don't know why, but I stood up.

Dr Waghorn's palms slid across the smooth grey sides of her head.

I sat back down. What this up and down was about, I haven't a clue.

"This is the thing," she told me with a long sigh. "I need your help with another student."

A sick feeling. A sagging. Already I didn't want this.

"What kind of help?" I asked and she put up a hand to stop me asking any more.

Did she sense my apprehension, hear my whining doubts even before I formed them? It must have all shown up on my poor red, sweaty face.

"Your term go well, did it? No problems?"

Why the pastoral now, for God's sake? It was clearly just an afterthought, an obligation. But I didn't want to talk about myself or waste any more time. I might have been awkward with adults, but I could read them well enough, particularly when they were as reluctant to talk about personal matters as she was.

"Everything was fine, thank you. What kind of help do you need from me?"

She raised an eyebrow, scratched a dry kneecap.

"You need to spend the night watching over some girl," she announced and breathed out at last.

I knew to wait now.

"She has to have someone with her at all times. There's a post-grad there now, an American called Hannah, I think, but she's been there since early afternoon and must be given a break. All it requires is that you sit with her until her parents arrive to pick her up and then you may go."

"Why?" I asked.

"Because she is . . . she *has* a history of wanting to . . . of wanting to end things. Do you understand?"

I didn't and I think maybe my mouth hung open because for a moment Dr Waghorn looked like she might even laugh at me.

"You're children, all of you," she complained.

"Does she want to kill herself?" I asked.

She pulled in her chin and eyed me, clearly amused by my bluntness.

"That's what she says – and she's said this kind of thing before and even attempted it. Her parents live very far North and will drive through the night to pick her up. I doubt they'll get here until the morning. In the meantime, I need someone to sit with her. I'm afraid that will have to be you."

"But," and I stopped at once, because I had so many objections that I didn't know where to start.

"Her name is Danielle Gartner. She's a year above you. Can't recall her subject. Do you know her?"

I shook my head. Danielle. I'd known two Danielles at school, one a bully, one vague and self-obsessed. I hadn't liked either. The name was pretty tarnished for me.

"I just have to sit with her?"

"That's all. I think that's pretty standard practice in these situations. I would do it myself but I am obliged to attend this foreign thing. It would look bad if I didn't go. Anyway, you're young, you can cope with a night of no sleep."

Could I? I didn't think I could.

"Because you mustn't doze off or anything. People like her can be very sly about things. They see it as a challenge."

"But what if she tries to do something?"

And now the gaunt hawk actually smiled. I think she pitied me.

"Oh, I doubt she will."

That wasn't quite good enough.

"But what if she does?"

Dr Waghorn waved the notion away impatiently.

"It's a game, probably. An indulgence. She's toying with us because she's bored or unhappy or thinks she's not getting the attention she deserves. I've heard her described variously as a genius and a weirdo. There are some people who are so excessively rational that they begin to question the point of themselves. Well, we've all done that at moments in our lives but most of us – of us *normal* people – just accept that things are the way they are and that we have to carry on. I dare say she'll feel the same way when she comes to her senses. In the meantime, we have to make sure she doesn't do anything stupid – or not on college property anyway."

I wanted to go back to my room and drink my Coke and watch my telly. I wanted the blank and the blamelessness of the end of another day. But I *was* curious, too, I have to admit. All this talk about *people like her* aroused in me a sense of thrilling jeopardy. My life experience was so limited at that point, my upbringing so happily dull and unremarkable, that I got a frisson of potential adventure out of the thought of this raving girl, this basket case, this victim who needed protecting from herself. And, of course, I was a little puffed up from Waghorn's opening remark, her relief that I was her only choice. She would have chosen me, had I been one of many.

I was already seen as a good person. A helpful type.

Dr Waghorn got up from her sofa, crossed her living room and disappeared into her kitchen. Was I supposed to go with her? Was the meeting over? But she was back in a moment, holding the stem of a glass which still contained a mouthful of red wine.

"I feel bad for this Hannah person, don't you?" she said, her tone almost confiding. "She's been there since about two."

I nodded because I understood that things – my respon-sibilities – were meant to be starting.

"The poor Yank needs a break now, don't you think?"

Once more, a nod, nothing verbal. I couldn't.

"Gartner's room is Hardiman Court, room sixteen, I believe. Ghastly building. I'd probably top myself as well if I had to live there. Brutalist monstrosity."

I wasn't grasping her, was hovering between getting up from my seat and staying put.

"Right, where are my bloody keys?" And she scanned the room, before her eyes came back to rest on mine. We paused, me suddenly bewildered by everything, her irked by my presence.

"Just one thing." She fixed me with that intense raptor stare. "They can be sneaky, people like her. Tricky. They beguile you."

"But why?" I asked her, backing towards her door.

"Because they want you to give them your approval. Your blessing. Your permission."

My back collided with her door and I froze.

"My permission?" My voice, even to my own ear, was tiny and childish.

"That's it. Let yourself out. Don't wait for me. I can't find my blasted keys. Best you go straight away, don't you think? Everything will be fine – just don't waste any more time. Your turn to be on watch."

And I pulled open her door and let myself out.

❦

The American postgrad answered the door and her angry relief came rushing out of her.

"Thank God!" she said, through her teeth, trying to keep her voice down. She pulled the door closed behind her. "I've just been abandoned here. I mean, what took you so long? I was told this was going to happen on a rota."

Strangely, I felt more cowed before this powerful, stocky, blonde young woman, than I had in the presence of the formidable Dr Waghorn.

"I'm sorry," I said.

"It's so boring," she complained, and the word dragged out of her. "I mean this kind of thing should be done by professionals, shouldn't it?"

The same thought had occurred me as I crossed the quad to get there. But I'd assumed that the danger of this Danielle girl doing herself any harm was probably slight and that if the parents just wanted her to have a companion through the night then they couldn't have been too worried. Waghorn had been overly dramatic. I would have to prepare myself for her disconcerting ways for when we *crossed swords*.

"Shall I go in?" I asked, stupidly.

"Well, *I'm* not going back," said the post-grad. "I wish I'd brought a book. Better than sitting in silence like that for hours."

And she left, outraged. I felt bad for her and then I felt bad for myself. I stood in front of Danielle Gartner's door and experienced an urge to walk away, to run after Hannah and let her berate me a little more. Better than the unknown. Better than the boredom that surely lay ahead of me. Why hadn't I brought a book?

But Dr Waghorn had been right about one thing. Luckily for her, one of the few students still there at the beginning of the summer holidays was a nineteen-year-old with a prevailing sense of responsibility. A girl who dearly wanted to prove herself an altruist.

I knocked on the door and went in.

2

SHE SAT ON her bed, her legs pulled up and held in her arms, and her chin on her kneecaps.

But I couldn't look at her.

What struck me was the unexpected emptiness of her room. I'd never seen an undergraduate's college quarters so plain and unadorned, so *unpacked*. Hardiman Court was a modern block (not quite as ghastly as Dr Waghorn had labelled it but not attractive either), mainly the preserve of second and third years. I'd been inside it before and been impressed by how tasteful and grown-up some of those rooms looked, with their cheese plants and film posters, brimming bookshelves and admirably cluttered desks.

There was nothing here but a bed, desk, wardrobe and armchair – and a cardboard box under the desk which, I assumed, contained all the items that should have been on it. The collapsing sun stood raw before a sealed, curtainless, window. The place was stifling and oppressive.

What do you say? What on earth do you say?

I remained at the door and waited and eventually I had no choice but to advance into the room. I couldn't look at her at that point, let alone say anything. I wonder if I thought she might break to pieces if I asserted myself in any way.

All I suddenly knew was that I had never been in such a situation and was not equipped for what was being asked of me.

"I can't open the window, sorry," I heard her say.

I looked up and saw a smile before anything else. A broad, apologetic smile.

I'd seen her before, now that I allowed myself to take her in. It wasn't such a huge college that you could remain anonymous for ever. Different years rarely mingled – it was like being at school in that regard – but certain faces always made a deeper scar in your memory and hers was one of them. All the same, there had been so little in common between us – evident in one glance – that I'd never really given her any thought.

Danielle Gartner straightened her legs and sat up against the wall and pushed her hair off her face and inspected me. I inspected her right back. What did she see? An awkward, pale-red-haired, bespectacled adolescent in her brother's football shorts and a washed-out mauve T-shirt. What did I see?

Or should I say, what did I *think* I saw? Because – and I know I keep saying this – I was nineteen. My world view was that of a schoolgirl. I had completed a year at university, but it might as well have been another year of school, only without my parents to run home to. I was unsophisticated, still a little damaged by the girl-pack experience, untried, untested. I might have thought I was worldlier than most but that was nonsense. I was a child.

And she wasn't.

Not that Danielle was an adult either, but someone hovering between the two states, at an optimal place for looking in both directions. I could tell at once that she understood more about everything than I did. It undid me. Within seconds of stepping through that door, I lost any plans I'd made on the way there to play the nurturing parent figure, someone who had the edge over her dependent.

But most of all I was caught out by her beauty.

She was slim though not at all thin and her skin was a warm brown, a few degrees lighter than her chestnut hair which was bobbed and curly and copious. Her eyebrows were broad and unkempt, which was the fashion of the day, and her eyes slightly protruding, very round, a little odd, rather dark. Her mouth was large but placid. Her smile was both glorious and outlandish.

She wore a chocolate brown silk dress with cream polka dots, and with a wide, loose neckline. She was – and this sounds so odd for me to have noticed – so healthy-looking, so flawless. I suppose I'd expected a wreck, someone who exuded failure and fear. But she looked like she might get up at any moment and head off to meet friends at a restaurant. I mean, who wears a dress like that during the day! For no reason, particularly no social reason, and without needing to be seen and approved of? And, come to that, why didn't I own such a perfect dress?

Her feet were bare and her toenails painted rose-petal pink.

For a moment this disparity in our appearances – particularly those impeccable little nails – infuriated me.

"I'd just got back from a run," I told her and threw myself into her armchair.

Her eyebrows shot up and she suppressed a laugh.

"I'm very sorry," she sympathised.

I mumbled something about it being too hot to run anyway.

"I don't have anything to drink, sorry," she apologised once more. Her voice was deeper than mine and more cultured. It was the same velvet tone as her skin and eyes. "I would go out and get some but I think I'm meant to stay where you can see me."

This last comment aggravated me even further. This whole arrangement seemed so farcically casual that I didn't see why she should feel so victimised.

"You can do what you like," I told her, ungraciously.

Another full, bizarre smile.

"I can indeed. Although it's not that easy. Doing what you like."

Did she mean what I thought she meant? I was appalled and not ready. I wasn't going to be drawn into that kind of conversation, that personal, psychological kind.

"Tell a lie," she suddenly said brightly, and pushed herself off her bed. "I've got this."

She walked rapidly to her door and was out of it before I knew what was happening. I leapt from the armchair and rushed into the corridor.

To my relief she was in the kitchen. Each floor of the Hardiman block had a communal kitchen with a fridge and cooker and food cupboards. I couldn't see this girl ever cooking, ever using the place at all. I imagined her food being brought to her, and her empty plates taken away. But she fished around in the fridge and stood upright and showed me a bottle of white wine and grinned.

"Don't worry," she confided, walking past me and back into her room. "I'll water it down nicely to make it last. It's going to be a long night."

※

"To the suicide watch," she said and raised her glass.

Too flippant, too soon, I thought.

I wasn't expecting her to say the word. We'd chatted a little

16

as she opened the bottle. I'd told her my name and I think we even complained about the heat and then I retreated to the armchair again, while she sat on the floor opposite me, her back against her bed, and poured the wine.

I reasoned that surely part of my role was to stop her thinking gloomy thoughts. (Oh God, that's how naïve I was.) If I could steer her away from any dark subject then I might instil a more positive vibe. But I was clueless about such things and besides I was still angry. She could – I'm sure – see the conflict not so deep inside me.

"Don't you have a telly?" I asked.

She shrugged with good-natured bewilderment.

"What about books then?"

"Oh. They're all at home."

"Don't you read in bed?"

Again, a friendly shake of the head.

"But for your course," I persisted. "Don't you need to read for your degree?"

"Of course I do."

That's it. That was our small talk. That's where anything trivial ended that night. She wasn't interested in the inconsequential. She didn't wish to fill time or populate silence with worthless words. I felt like I could cast away anything frivolous and immaterial. I was too young and inexpert at decoy chatter, in any case. I wanted to know things. I wanted to confront her there and then and let her know how I felt about being there.

Danielle Gartner dropped her chin to her chest and left me for a moment. The top of her head was thick with dark curls, hair so utterly different to my lank, sallow strands that I wondered if we were even the same species. I waited for her to speak but nothing came and so I looked around her room and, with nothing of interest there either, felt the ire rise even higher. Well, I thought, if you can be so unblinkingly direct, so could I.

"Why are you doing this?" I asked. "Aren't you worried that you'll upset your family?"

For a moment there was nothing but silence between us. I was to get used to this, this waiting for an answer. She never seemed spontaneous, always gave even the most throwaway question thorough consideration.

"Are you sure you want to have this conversation?"

"Well I haven't had any choice in anything so far, have I?" I came back, fast and with feeling.

"I'm sorry," she mumbled. "I was an idiot. I said something I shouldn't have. It's ruined your evening."

"But your family," I pushed. "Aren't you ruining *their* evening, too?"

"Am I?"

Such a monstrously stupid and insensitive question. What was she playing at? Was she trying to get me to say repellent things? Well, I wouldn't. I wasn't going to say those words she found so easy to utter.

"Yeah, you are, you really are. They're probably really worried about you. You're their child."

"Oh, I see." And another pause before: "When do I stop being their child, do you think? When can I make decisions about myself without worrying that I might hurt them?"

"Never," I said at once.

"That can't be right. It can't be. That would be too cruel."

"You're the one who's being cruel," I insisted. "Playing these games."

18

Naturally, she thought about this too.

"Why do you say I play games? I've long grown out of playing games."

So I drank my wine and muttered into my glass, although I was already loosening a little, maybe because of the alcohol, maybe because she had seemed so substantial and not at all the bundle of fizzing nerve ends I'd expected. If anyone had walked into that room just then and been asked to point out the self-harming neurotic, I suspect they would have gone for me.

I was always too proud in those days, too combative. Too ready for a fight. I felt I had to assert myself from the start. I had a ton of chips on my shoulders. But I sensed early on there was going to be no easy route to self-righteousness with this one. Would she care that I was from what I so readily described as a working-class home? That I went to a comprehensive school? That I wasn't pretty or imposing or outstanding in any way? My schtick was that I worked hard, never went easy on myself. That's what got me to the university. But would that even register?

She wasn't aloof or superior in any way. But she wasn't like me, either. I didn't see any fight in her. I saw a kind of peace which suggested she was well beyond the need to fight, that she knew things I didn't. Maybe that's what I'd mistaken for beauty, that composure.

Now and then I'd given some thought to physical beauty in the abstract. Not having much of it myself, it intrigued me. Was it even useful? What advantage did girls like Danielle Gartner have over me? It was all just an accident, surely. I didn't hold with the notion that beauty led to a better mate. Maybe an equally beautiful mate but not a better human.

Everybody had the same run-up to procreation, whatever their appearance, and babies appeared out of the wombs of even the most unappealing mothers. And so maybe beauty had no biological use at all – it was merely a random falling of the features in a particular way. People like me liked to look at people like her in the same way that we'd enjoy a painting or a view. Which was probably why rich men married beautiful women, I guessed – because they could have them to themselves and look at them all the time.

How awful to be looked at all the time.

"Why don't you take your trainers off?" she said. "Your feet must be sweltering."

I glanced at her petal nails. I would not remove my trainers.

"So how come you're still here after the end of term?" I asked.

"Why are *you* still here?"

"Because my parents have gone abroad and they're having the house redecorated while they're away and I've got nowhere to go for a few days. Anyway, I don't mind being here alone."

She seemed to approve of my answer.

"Neither do I. I pretended I had a summer course so I could be alone for a while."

"English," she then said. "I've got you down as an English student. Am I right?"

"No," I told her. "Economics. But not for long. Changing to Social and Political Sciences."

She shook her head slowly.

"Social and Political Sciences. Didn't see that one."

"What about you?"

"Theology."

She might as well have told me she was a fascist.

"You're not religious, are you?" I demanded, scandalised.

There was only a year between us but it might have been a lifetime. All I seemed to do was snort and stamp my feet like a child.

"You don't have to be religious to study theology," she replied simply.

"I thought you did."

"No."

I wasn't letting go.

"So, why are you studying it then?"

"It's the only subject that interests me. It *is* very interesting."

"Is it?"

"Yes. You know how they say Latin helps you understand other languages? Well, I think theology helps you understand other things too. Informs us."

"About how stupid we are," I huffed.

She pursed her mouth against smiling.

"Very possibly," she said and politely gave it some though

Suddenly she got up and walked to the window, her profile instantly ignited in red. She put her face in her hands and stood like that for a while, sunken, profoundly apart from me, the sunset blazing around her. I couldn't have reached her if I tried.

What did Dr Waghorn expect of me? She should have given more specific instructions. Was I supposed to soothe this girl, keep talking at her until either the dawn came up and her parents arrived or she forgot why we were all there in the first place? I must have had some practical use in this scenario but I couldn't work out what it was.

Her hands dropped from her face and she was looking

intently at something or someone in the grounds. We were four floors up and surrounded by parkland. At this time in the evening during the summer holidays, tourists were allowed to visit the college park and gardens. The going opinion was that they shuffled through like cattle but I always thought we were the cattle, grazing in our enclosures, watching the strangers pass through, wondering where they came from and where on earth they went.

"SPS is interesting, too. And very useful," I said.

"What?" she asked, and her eyes darted about to find where the voice had come from.

"Some degrees are useful and some aren't. I wasn't going to waste my time on something that wouldn't benefit me later. That's why I changed."

"Oh," she said and made her way back to her bed, perching on the edge of it.

"You've got it all planned out, have you?"

"I certainly have."

I straightened up. If this was the way things were going then I could easily keep it up. I had a whole life plan to lay before her.

"I know what I'm doing when I leave here. I've worked it all out. First of all – "

"Shall we go out?" she said. "It's unbearably hot in here."

Panic arrived before I even recognised what it was.

"I can't," I told her. "We can't."

"Says who?" she laughed.

"We're to stay here."

"Listen," she said to me and I still hear her saying it, the placid authority, the hand hovering near my arm. I hear her saying it over the thirty years that separate then and now, and

I remember the pale gold hairs against the sun-tanned skin, the little white bone tip at her wrist.

"You don't really think you can stop me doing what I'm going to do, do you?" And she was delivering the sunniest smile as she said it. "I told you I don't play games."

3

I WAS RUNNING down the stairs behind her, catching sight only of a flap of her dress as it disappeared around each corner.

I didn't even understand how it happened. One minute she'd been talking to me about her course, which lecturers she admired, which she hated, all the while rummaging under her bed for her sandals and strapping them on to her feet, the next she was out of the door.

I felt terror at first and then the whip crack of urgency, but even that brief dithering gave her a considerable head start.

"Hang on!" I'd called. Then: "Shit! Shit! Shit!"

But at the bottom of the stairs she was waiting for me, simply standing at the entrance and looking out into the park. How had it got dark that quickly? From where we stood, we could see in the middle distance the old buildings, where I had my own room, and where I'd been to see Dr Waghorn. Hardiman Court was separated from these by parkland, a path cutting through it, busy during term with students crossing from home to college, deserted now. The path was bordered on one side by a high brick wall which separated us from the town and on the other by the river.

It was with dismay that I watched her step out from the entrance and head towards the river.

"Where are you going?" I called, already losing her to the dark.

"Come on, keep up," wafted back to me.

She wasn't trying to get away from me, I realised. What on earth was I thinking? That she'd take a running jump at the water?

That's exactly what I was thinking.

But I also got a sense that she actually wanted me with her and that my company was perhaps a little entertaining. Could it be that I was making her think about things? That my anger and vehemence, my appeal to her through her suffering parents, had penetrated? Had I reached her heart quite that readily? Well! Wasn't I something!

Looking back, I really think I was that pompous, even when on the backfoot. My job had been to watch over her but already I was warming up to the role of saviour.

I reached her side and together we found our way down to the riverside. There was no one anywhere near us, although there were some lighted windows in the old college buildings further up the path.

"Be careful," I told her. She was very near the edge of the water now, looking into its routine darkness.

To my relief, I saw she was sitting down. This stretch of river was very civilised and tamed. The grass was regularly mown and the river bank itself as neat and accommodating as a made bed. She was removing her sandals and putting her feet in the water.

"Ah, that's better," she said. "Come on. Look, it's so dark, it looks like your feet are cut off at the ankles."

I shook my head and grumbled – didn't care for her way of describing things – or about the dance she was leading me on.

"Why didn't I bring the wine?" she complained.

I stood above her and looked down at her head, saw the

faint white line of her parting, a tiny path. One shoulder was bare where her wide collar had slipped.

And so I got down beside her and, still grumbling, removed my trainers and socks and gingerly introduced my feet to the cold, lost them, like she had, to the dark.

"Bingo," she said.

"What?" I asked. While it felt unquestionably good to have my feet in cold water, I was still in a state of panic over what she might do next.

"That's all I wanted, to get you to take your bloody trainers off."

"That's why we're here? For my feet?"

"Yes! That's why we're here." And she dropped her head back and inhaled the night and seemed utterly content with the way things had worked out.

"You're not supposed to be outside. You're meant to stay in your room," I chided.

"Why?"

I didn't really know and the question escaped from me, with no answer to catch hold of it.

"You'll get your dress wet," I tried.

"So?"

I was back to my frustration, my flailing fear of inadequacy.

"It's all right for people like you," I informed her and the hectoring began. "Posh people just do what they want, feel like they're born to it. The rest of us aren't so comfortable in places like this."

She lifted her head and turned her face to mine with wide eyes and lips dancing with mirth.

"Oh, I'm posh, am I?"

"Yes. You clearly are."

"And how do you work that out?"

"Just look at you. The way you dress. The way you speak. Studying theology just for fun, because you feel like it. You know what that is? That's bourgeois."

(It was the 1980s. I was young. Forgive me.)

She knew not to goad me by laughing but she was, of course, revelling in my audacity.

I needed to say more (dear God.)

"My dad's a builder and my mum works in a shop," I told her by way of supplying her with my non-bourgeois credentials. "I grew up in a terraced house in South London. That's the world I come from."

She gave it some thought, looking me fondly and directly in the face as she did so.

"You're right. I don't know anything of that world. That's not my background at all."

I should have felt satisfied but I wasn't particularly. As usual, as my moral indignation subsided, so my shame welled up.

"I'm an army brat," she told me, returning to face the blank of the river. "My dad's a soldier, an officer but not particularly high-ranking. My mum doesn't work. We've moved around a lot. I'm not especially posh – I suppose I just talk like my mother. But I'm not really bothered about that kind of thing. Who cares what people think about your accent? Oh and why shouldn't I study a subject that interests me? Are you suggesting that we should only chose our subjects on pragmatic grounds?"

"I think taxpayers would rather we did," I snapped back. "They don't care whether you believe in God or not."

"Oh, we're back to that, are we? You hate the thought that

I might be a God-botherer. Bad enough that you're wasting your time with a nutter, let alone a religious nutter."

And it's at that point, I think, with our feet cooling, our hands resting on the grass, that I stopped fighting her. Because she already knew what I thought and what I felt and there was no way of surprising her either with my intellect or my politics. She understood it all. And I had nothing left.

Was Waghorn right? Had she beguiled me? I really didn't think so. She had no need to trap me or trick me into saying or doing anything. All she had done was to have stung me, and a little of her exceptional venom was now in my system, altering my make-up, adapting me to her. I could scold her and lecture her, I could mock her and argue with her, but I might as well have been nagging the sky for being too high, too beyond my reach. Better to try and understand.

"Don't read too much into it," she said casually. "Theology is just like history with some psychology on the side."

"I suppose so," I conceded.

"I'm very interested in the earliest appearances of worship. Prehistoric religion. At what point in the development of our brains did we think: oh I can't take any more of this unpredictable shit – I need someone who I can blame, who can be responsible."

"Why?"

"Because the world kept wrong-footing us."

"No, I mean why does that interest you?"

"Oh," she said. "Why. I see. Good question. Because there is a bit of those early brains in all of us, I suppose."

"Not in me," I told her airily.

"Yes, in you. In me. In everyone. We haven't changed an iota. It was a lottery then and it's a lottery now."

"We don't need gods now," I said.

"Don't we? I think you'll find we have exactly the same craving for perfection that we had then. Maybe the questions are more sophisticated but we're still peering into the clouds for answers. We still want to know if we are loved by someone or something. If it really matters whether we live or die."

Once again, Waghorn's words were drifting back into my mind. *They begin to question the point of themselves.* She had made it sound so throwaway, so callow. But Danielle wasn't like the girls at my old school who claimed to be depressed or who needed reassurance. I was in the presence of something different, more demanding of my comprehension. I couldn't bustle in and put her right, like I had others. And Waghorn clearly didn't have a clue, either.

I so wanted to understand her. To engage with her on this. I wanted to impress her, too. But of course, I didn't want to upset her and in the end, I could see, it would be best to tie off this conversation and move onto less treacherous ground.

"Well, if nothing else we have a biological purpose," I said. "Instinct. We have it in us to nurture our young. There's nothing complicated in that."

She didn't answer me at once and I could see that she was swallowing, like she had a bad taste in her mouth. Her expression seemed embittered, the corners of her mouth turned down, her shoulders stiff and tense.

"Yes," she said eventually and faintly. "Yes, we have. You're quite right. The rest is extraneous."

I can pursue this or I can knock it on the head, I thought.

"What will you do?" I suddenly asked her. "With your life, I mean? What kind of job awaits you?"

This was my favourite topic of conversation – the

barely-concealed excitement that accompanied speculation over future employment.

And I realised at once what I'd done and put a hand to my mouth in childish shock.

She dropped backwards into the grass, her face turned up to the night, her hair falling among the grass stalks.

"It's alright," she reassured me. "I'm the strange one, not you. Never feel awkward asking me such things, but the truth is I can't answer you. Not because I don't have an answer but because you won't like my answer. I made the mistake once of confiding to my sister and that's why you're here now, because a lot of things were put in motion then and people who call themselves professionals took an interest in me, which I find revolting by the way. Anyway, they listen out for things I say, so-called trigger words, and I must have triggered something talking to my supervisor on the phone this morning because that's why my parents are coming and that's why you're here when you could be watching the telly or reading in your bed."

"I don't mind!" I said at once.

I turned and lay on my stomach, the tips of my toes now the only part of me in the water. With my head twisted to the side and resting on my folded arms I could keep her in my sight, without having her look back at me. Her profile was soft now, seemed to be evaporating into darkness. Her lips, lashes, nose all frayed and disappearing.

Without her knowing – I *hoped* she didn't know – I let my fingers walk to the nearest curl as it lay in the grass and, gently as I possibly could, touched it. My heart beat faster as fingertip met hair.

She spoke.

"I like you far too much to bore you. I'd rather hear about your future plans, to be honest."

"You have to be careful," I told her with a new zeal. "You mustn't give them their trigger words. Don't give them the satisfaction."

(I ought to explain that I was very anti-authoritarian in those days and loved nothing more than a story of the little person fighting the system. I'm not going to keep apologising for my crassness. We were all young once.)

"I will be careful," she promised.

"Danielle," I asked, newly courageous. "Can I ask? Have you tried? Before, I mean?"

I moved my hand away from her hair.

"Like I said, I won't put you through this."

But I was struggling then with grasping how this striking, vital, extraordinary girl could really be what she was telling me she was: an ending. Nothing but an ending.

Beneath that exquisite dress was a strong young body, with all the potential of youth, the readiness to be loved and lusted over. If nothing else, the potential to have sex, surely. Didn't that drive us all? Particularly at that age?

The water was so still it was silent. The air so heavy it didn't move.

"I put myself to sleep. All right? Is that enough to know?"

She sat up suddenly and gathered her knees to her chest, and remained, closed up like that, just as I'd first seen her on her bed.

"And you really wanted to . . . well, to go to sleep?"

"This is not a topic of conversation," she said. "You can't make questions and sentences out of it. Or at least I can't

31

satisfy those questions. But why do you think I wouldn't want to?"

I let out a gasp.

"Look at you! Why *would* you? There's no reason."

"There's always a reason," she came back sharply. "It might be incomprehensible. It might be reprehensible. But there's always a bloody reason."

It was the first time she had shown me any fire and I was duly cowed.

When her voice returned it was genial again.

"I love how blunt you are," she said.

"I was thinking the same thing about you."

"You dare to tell me off. Others don't."

"You need a bloody good telling off!"

Still closed up, nose to knees, she spoke to me, and I heard her voice from a distance, as though we might be sitting miles apart.

"Listen," she told me, not a jot of anguish, not a hint of drama. "It's not a case of whether I will do it, but when. Knowing that simple fact should reassure you just as much as it does me."

4

WE WALKED THROUGH the unlit park towards the student residence, our bare, wet feet bouncing on the cool, mown grass, our shoes in our hands, and she did something that threw me. She put her arm around my shoulders. It was a spontaneous gesture on her part, but I shivered as soon as the arm landed and stiffened under it.

I knew what had prompted it.

"Come on," I told her, as we got up from the riverbank. "Let's get you safely indoors."

I had attempted to mother her and she'd been so touched and entertained by this moment of compassion that she'd needed to attach herself to me. But I was uncomfortable with such physical tokens. After a few steps I slipped myself from her arm as naturally as I could without – I hoped – causing offence and positioned myself behind her, where I could keep her entirely in my sights.

That's how we went up the four flights of stairs to her rooms, me bringing up the rear, and how we arrived back in that furnace of a sealed cell.

"Oh God, I wish we could open a window. I can barely breathe in here," she said. She stalked across the room and started working at the latch.

"No!" I cried. "You can't. You're not allowed."

She grit her teeth, jammed her palm under the latch and jabbed upwards.

"When do we stop caring about what we're allowed and not allowed to do?"

I was watching her with growing concern, hovering stupidly as she rammed her fist against the lock.

"I mean, I thought I was a free agent by now. It's not like I like I'm at home any more."

"Please stop," I begged. "Let's just keep the door open."

"I know!" she announced. "Come on."

And she was out of the door once again, me behind her.

I followed her to the little kitchen and watched her fetch two chairs from against the wall and position them by the fridge. She opened the fridge door and we settled in front of it, the confined, sterile air piling out of it and landing on our hot skin. Our eyes were drawn to that empty, lit box, as keenly as if it were a cinema screen.

"That's better," she said.

I felt at last that I could scold her.

"You mustn't go off and do anything again without telling me first. All right?"

෴

I asked Danielle about her family, as we sat there and stared, as one, into the fridge.

She told me about her two brothers and one sister. I asked if they were close and got on well. She shrugged. "Yeah, I suppose," she said. "I'm the youngest, so they really love me and they're really scared of me."

I told her about my own big brother and how inseparable we'd been when little, how distant now.

"And your parents?" I asked. "Do you get on with them?"

(I stole a quick glance at her profile.)

"My parents are wonderful," she told me. "They're devoted to us."

Then why break their hearts like this! I was appalled at how detached she seemed.

"What's your house like?" I went on, wanting to talk about my own.

"We've moved about a lot," she answered. "We don't seem to get attached to things very much. We always rent. My dad's retiring soon and they'll probably get something nice with his pension. Just right for the two of them. I hope so. My mum deserves a permanent garden. Not that a garden is ever permanent, don't you think?"

No idea. My turn.

"My parents don't stop travelling. Ever. They're probably trying to get away from me."

"Aren't all parents trying to get away from their kids?"

"Too deep! Moving on . . ."

She laughed.

"Can't I say anything?"

"Nothing meaningful, no. Don't you ever just talk crap?"

"I try," she smiled.

"Well, try harder."

"I just meant that being a parent must be so painful. So painful and yet so beautiful. You're tied to another human for the rest of your days. It obliterates everything else. You must want to escape just to be able to breathe. And then, if you do, you want to feel that tie again. You don't ever want to undo that knot."

"I don't think my parents feel particularly tied to me."

"Really? I bet they are."

"And I can't imagine I'll ever be a mum. Or not a good one anyway."

She seemed knowledgeable on these things in a way that I most definitely was not.

"You probably will. And if your parents loved you then you'll probably be the same kind of loving parent."

I didn't really want to talk about my parents – felt a little peeved with them the more I did – and so I let the subject lapse.

I realised in the silence that followed that it was late, around midnight, and that I was tired. It hadn't occurred to me until that point. When would we sleep? And if she slept, did I have to be awake to guard her? I glimpsed at her face and found it revealed absolutely no signs of fatigue. Her dark eyes were alive with the fridge light, her skin sheeny.

"So," she said and dropped her legs to the floor and turned to look squarely at me. "Tell me all about it."

I had no idea what she was alluding to. It felt like I'd been found out.

"What?" I asked. "What do you want to know?"

"The life plan. You said earlier than you had it all mapped out. I'm curious. Go on, hit me with it."

"What, now?"

"Yes now."

I flapped. "But you're not interested in that."

"I most certainly am. Like you, I'd rather not talk about motherhood."

She faced the fridge once more, put her feet up next to mine on the bottom edge. Twenty toes in a row, exactly level. How had we arrived here, Danielle and I, at a point where anyone watching would see comfortable friendship, love even?

We had known each other for only four hours.

"Don't laugh," I told her, my heartbeat quickening.

"I'll laugh if it's funny," she insisted.

"It's not funny. It's serious."

"Well go on then. I think we're about to break the fridge."

I looked at the perfection of her rose-pink nails and the ragged straight cut of my own. Would she ever understand a person like me, a lesser person, a duller one?

"I only really have one ambition," I told her.

"And that is?"

And so I said it.

"To do good."

And I winced. Possibly even ducked my head.

Danielle Gartner nodded slowly.

I turned to her in excitement.

"It's not just words, you know. I genuinely, honestly want to do some good with my life. And I know how I'll do it."

"How?" she asked.

"I'm going to work really hard and when I leave here, I'm going to train as a journalist – no hear me out – and from there I'm going to go into local politics and from there I'm going to stand for Parliament and I'm going to be an MP and change things. Because that's the only way you *can*. By getting hold of a little bit of power and influence and using it for good."

"There's no other way?"

"I've thought about it, and no, there isn't. Yeah, you can work for charities and look after old people and do all that kind of thing, but it's making decisions, difficult decisions from a point of authority, that's what changes society. That's the only way. Power isn't a dirty word if it's used for good."

That same – by now familiar – pursing of the lips while pondering.

"I don't understand why you have to be a journalist."

"Two reasons," I said, warming to the conversation at last, positively relishing it. "Because I believe that politicians have to go out into the world first and learn about it and know what's going on, and because working in news is the best way of doing it, I reckon. I could be a lawyer, but I don't think it's right for me."

"All right."

My nerves were jolting and little tremors were going off all over me, like pre-set detonations. It always happened when I unboxed the life-plan.

"I'm interested in your idea of doing good," she said. "What is doing good? Is it *being* good?

"No!" I told her hotly. "No. I'm not a saint. I'm angry. I'm angry about inequality and injustice. I don't want to sit by and accept things. I want to make a difference. A big difference."

"Yes, I understand," she said calmly, "but I still want to know what you mean by good. What is good?"

"It's helping other people, doing things for wider society, I suppose." I didn't see what she found so difficult to grasp.

"But is that good, I mean in the true moral sense of the word?"

"Yes!" I insisted. I had the speech to hand. "It's devoting your life to change. It's giving everything you've got, every ambition, every drop of energy, to getting a job done and keeping your eyes on the goal – bettering society."

"Ah, so that's good? Public service."

"Yes!"

"And is it still an act of goodness if people know you're doing it?" she ruminated.

"What do you mean?"

"Well, I mean, might you not be doing it for recognition? Do you want to be admired?"

I was a little stung but far from caught out. I should have known her motives were not to upset me or find cracks in my philosophy but simply to get at a truth. On this subject, however, I could be very touchy.

"You think this is an ego trip," I accused her.

"Well, we're all egos, aren't we? That's normal. Nothing wrong with that. You just got me thinking, that's all, about doing good. Sounds so simple. I wonder if it is."

"It *is* if it's effective." I pressed home my advantage. "I mean, if it's effective, then it's good."

"So, it's not about selflessness?"

Jesus! I thought. No one had been this challenging about my life plan before. Normally I just got plaudits. And a warm feeling of worth.

"Yes, selflessness comes into it," I told her. "It has to. Otherwise, how can you serve society?"

"And changing one life for the better is not good enough? It has to be society?"

"No," I said adamantly. "I mean – yes. I don't hold with all that 'as long as I'm a good parent and bring up good children' crap. That's not enough. Nothing changes that way. And doing a bit of voluntary work is totally a gesture and no more. It's just a ripple that disappears. You have to do something seismic."

I was searching her face for recognition. I wanted her applause. I needed the familiar accolades and the compliments.

Or maybe merely the shared excitement. But she still seemed distant, unconvinced.

"What's so wrong with society, anyway?" she asked me.

And she got up and pushed the fridge door shut.

By now it was second nature to me to mirror her moves. I stood beside her.

"What's wrong with society? Bloody hell, where do I begin!"

We walked back to the corridor and along it to her room. She went directly to the window and started struggling with the latch once more.

Meanwhile, I sat on her bed and proceeded to list all the ills of society as I saw them then, starting with the prime minister and including everything from the miners' strike, race riots, to run-down council housing and colonial-era foreign policy. I was in my element. I railed about underpaid workers, side-lined women, class privilege and educational inequality.

"Ah, that's it!" she said and flung open the window. She turned to me: "And you really think that you could change all that?"

I stood in terror and held out an arm. Dear God, the window was open. How did she do it?

"Danielle, get away from there," I gasped.

"Why?" she asked innocently.

"Because . . ."

We faced each other, dumb and uncomprehending.

"Oh!" she exclaimed at last. "Oh, I see! You thought I was going to leap from it. How funny! Well, you've put the idea in my head now."

I felt my legs soften.

"I'm joking," she laughed. "Don't worry. I just want some

fresh air, that's all. Come on. Come here beside me. You can see the clock tower from here. It's nearly 2am."

And so we stood side by side, leaning out of the window, bathing in the tepid night air (it was far from fresh), our bare arms sticking to each other's, our friendship stronger in that moment than any I had built over the years with girls from my childhood. I think we must have stood there for nearly an hour, chatting happily about all the issues I had raised, and she asked me questions and prompted answers that I thought were far cleverer than any I had ever produced before. It dawned on me that this was true intellectual rigour, to face unpartisan logic and to hand a different logic straight back.

But Danielle seemed to be travelling somewhere beyond my own dreams, to a place that ignited something in her imagination. Something that had promise and – dare I think it? – a future. Her voice, in its new fragility, suggested to me that she might be utterly captivated.

Or slightly pissed. We'd finished the wine and found and shared seven Baileys miniatures, a present, she said, from her sister, who sent Danielle small hampers consisting of booze, make-up and face creams. She dug out the stash from the bottom of her wardrobe and we proceeded to tip the contents of those little bottles down each other's throats and into our empty stomachs, solemnly, like we were conferring benedictions.

"A soupçon more, mademoiselle?" she asked with the last one.

"Yep," I said, and as she put it to my lips, her eyes on mine, I had felt an urge to cry. My mouth bubbled with intense feeling and I took the tiny bottle out of her hands.

"I don't make friends easily," I told her suddenly, surprising

41

myself. I said it as a confession and as a revelation. I said it out of gratitude.

She pulled back from me and her eyes searched my face.

"Well, that makes two of us, then." And she lifted a hand to my cheek, perhaps to pat it, or to stroke it. But I didn't feel it touch my skin.

"No crying, little Commie," she told me. "You'll be bloody useless if you fall to pieces every ten minutes."

Which, of course, made me want to cry all the more. Made me want to be held.

She was untouchable and yet begged to be touched, would be an island caressed by a sea of lovers one day, surely.

Danielle moved away from the window and paced round and round her room, singing under her breath. I turned my back on the sky and watched her.

Oh, my goodness but she was so radiant then. So celestial-seeming.

They beguile you.

But no, I had beguiled *her*, I was sure of it.

"To have a plan is a wonderful thing," she exclaimed. "And you have a most wonderful plan. A most wonderful, wonderful plan."

I stepped quickly into her path, got swept up, and we walked around the room together, in a tight circle that felt to me like exquisite madness. Why were we even doing it? We were giggling and panting with the effort. We were hypnotising ourselves.

And then she stopped and stamped her foot and dropped back her head and cried out to the ceiling.

"But what does it *mean* to be good?"

I was very hot, perspiring, and still laughing. I didn't understand her.

"Just . . . just good. Honestly. What don't you understand about good?"

"If you strip away all the behave-yourself morality, which is nicked from civic society in any case, then what's left? An instinct to do the right thing? How do we know what the right thing is? Is it, do you think, the individual's yearning to be godlike?"

I sat heavily down onto the edge of her bed and shook my head dramatically.

"What! Why bring God into it? You're obsessed, woman."

"I am, aren't I?"

But she stood before me, daring me to go on, wanting to have this out, regardless of how exhausted we were.

"It gives me the heebie-jeebies to think of you studying God all the time."

"Gods."

"Gods, whatever. I can't think why people like gods. They're awful, controlling things. They treat humans like children that can't think for themselves."

She clapped at that.

"You see! You're virtually a theologian, talking like that. No, what gets me, is – what's in it for the gods? It must be bleak, living for ever, controlling people's lives, never really living for yourself. What do they get out of it?"

"I dunno. Eternal smugness? At least with humans, the children grow up and go away. A god can never let his guard down. He's not a father – he's an omnifather."

"Awful. We should feel sorry for them."

"I'm being sexist. I mean, an omnimother."

"An omnimother," she considered. "She who sees all, knows all, controls all, and there's absolutely nothing in it for her."

"Except the knowledge that all her children – all the ones who believe in her, of course – are exceptional and will worship her for ever."

"Maybe she doesn't want to be worshipped," Danielle said. "Maybe she's just happy to watch over them. Maybe she just loves them. Maybe blind, instinctive love is a million times more powerful than goodness."

I still had a lecture in me, a soapbox moment on how there wasn't anything in the slightest godlike or supernatural about being able to make changes that might spread a little wealth in society. Or improve education, or make sure people got good jobs. How, with some will and energy and, of course, influence, the lot of others could be improved. But I was desperately tired and losing my sparse oratory powers. Instead, I told her:

"I don't want to be a god. I don't care about definitions of good. I just want to have a go at changing things so that people who are born poor might not have to go through life poor. And people who are different might not be made to feel different. Or something like that. I feel a bit sick."

It was almost in a whisper that she said:

"Then you must. It's as simple as that."

She returned to the window and looked away into the near dawn. At long last the air was cooling, the heat dissipating. The breeze lifted the hair from her temples and I marvelled at the tight baby curls that framed her hairline. How perfect and unearthly she seemed to me then, a drawn girl, an ideal, a dream of a human. How unlike me.

I watched the eyebrow nearest me shoot up to presage a new question.

"And I suppose the more common ambitions, to fall in love and live happily ever after don't figure in your plan?"

I grinned.

"Why not? I want all those things. I can be an MP and still have a happy relationship, can't I?"

"Be in love?"

"God yeah! Just watch me."

"Well," she said, "it really does seem like you've worked it all out."

"I so want to fall in love, don't you?" I told her. "And I can see him already. He'll be really clever, first of all, but really good-looking, too. I'll probably meet him at work. We will be devoted to each other. And fancy each other till the day we die. I'm not interested in the students here, they're like kids. I want a man. Oh, and he must share my politics. Our marriage will be part love story, part mission. We'll do this together."

She was looking at me intently.

Her eyes were unearthly, dark, imperious, but her expression was almost stupefied. Her neck was rigid, her body taut. Something had happened. She was transfixed, her features petrified.

"What is it?" I asked, getting up from the bed and peering at her.

She remained rooted to the floor, her eyes still mining into mine.

"Danielle, are you all right? You look funny."

Should I slap her? It never occurred to me that she might have funny turns or be incapacitated.

"Please, please," I begged her. "Tell me what's wrong?"

Her hands lifted slowly and arrived either side of my face. Her gaze couldn't be more powerful than at that moment. Never in my life had I felt so examined and so thoroughly understood.

"I want to give you something," she said.

Her face was so close to mine. I didn't understand what she was offering me.

"What?" I asked her.

Her lips were slightly apart, her breath audible in that close and humid room.

"What?" I repeated.

She didn't reply.

Very gently, very precisely, I removed myself from her hands, stepped back.

"A cheque will do nicely," I said, trying to lighten whatever it was that had suddenly materialised between us.

Her arms dropped to her sides and her body sagged a little. Her faint, preoccupied smile reminded me of how my mother used to look, tidying up the mess in my bedroom every evening. The secret smile of sacrifice.

"You must be knackered," I told her. "Any chance we could just stop now?"

I fell onto her bed and instantly, responding to an urge I had not been aware of until then, curled up and put my hands under my cheek.

I felt the end of the bed give as she landed on it and looked up to find her positioned exactly as I'd first seen her, back against the wall, legs pulled up, chin on knees, hair over her eyes. I released one of my hands and took hold of the hem of her dress so that if she tried to escape, I'd feel it.

I was comfortable, relieved and quietly elated, and at that moment I didn't believe in any nastiness or failure or weakness. We were brimming with strength and wisdom. We were exceptional people.

"Oh Danielle, isn't it fantastic? All of it."

46

"What's that?" she murmured, as distracted as I was.

"All the unknown, all the delicious unknown. How awful it will be one day to be looking back on it all and not now, looking ahead."

And then things just became calmer and mellower, and the periods of silence lengthened. With the minute drop in temperature came a bodily relaxation, an overwhelming need to give up and give in, to let my energies dwindle and to slowly shut down. I lay with my head at her feet, a curled-up thing, an insect, pacified, come to its end. Sometimes she hummed and, when she did, I felt myself smile.

The temperature was no longer oppressive, the air was lighter and kinder. The night was over. We had reached that pure and splendid moment of the day that was a new starting-point. It could go anywhere.

"Danielle," I said, my eyes closed, my body entirely torpid, sleep moments away.

"Yes?" came the voice.

"Isn't it beautiful?" I told her. "The sun coming up."

She didn't answer.

"We've done it. We've got through the night."

Still nothing.

"It's dawn. Your parents will be here soon and you can recover, and everything will be all right."

From now on I would always stay up for the dawn (I actually believed that) and perhaps I would offer my services to the college to look after other troubled students. Because I was capable and responsible, a caring kind of person, the type the college authorities talked about and made note of and trusted. I'd kept watch over this girl all night and now the morning was here and we were both free.

I felt the merest kiss of her hand on my hair and it was like a switch. I had to sleep now, could barely move my head to look at her, didn't need to: she was there, sitting upright, facing an empty room, surely as sleep-starved as I was.

I had kept watch.

I had kept her alive.

But this is what I heard her say – and I heard it like it was coming from some other place, miles from that bed, barely audible because of its distance:

"I hate the dawn. When I wake up in the morning, I wish with all my heart that I was still asleep. And then I feel my pulse and I can't help it, I start to cry.

"Every morning – just lying there – I have only one hope: that somehow or other this might be my last morning. But then another one comes, and another, and another.

"Because it's unbearable. It hurts so much. I can't endure any more of it. It's an illness. It's an allergy! I don't expect you to understand me. I'm glad you don't."

Her words, so sharp and painful, came out as unremarkable fact. *Nothing will change for me*, she was saying. *This is what I am.*

And I understood and accepted. This was how she was. I had kept her intact for one more day. That was all.

"Thank you," I heard her say. "Thank you for staying with me all night. And now you'd better go out and live your life."

I AWOKE IN the late morning heat.
The room was empty and the window wide open.

PART TWO

1

THE FIRST HOME I ever owned was a comically mi-
niscule four-room flat folded into the eves of a Victorian
villa in a woody village of South East London. It cost my
father £30,000 all in. I still smile at that figure and tell my
children about it. What can you get for thirty thousand in
London now? It must have been horrible, they say, no more
than a cupboard, an awkward little pit.

But it wasn't. It was lovely. The house was up on a hill and,
though the area was classed as Inner London, I could see the
bubbling green mass of North Kent from the porthole that
was my bedroom window. Once upon a time, the building
had been the imposing property of a very wealthy family, who
had quartered their servants on site in their own bedrooms.
But my flat wasn't even part of the old servant's wing. It was
higher than that. It had been hewn out of the attic space and
so my ceilings finished in points and it felt like I was hiding
out in a tiny church. A tiny church up in the air.

My parents had sold the family home in Gipsy Hill to
finance their travel plans and gave my brother and me enough
to invest in property. My brother lived in Manchester and
bought a two-bedroomed terraced house with his cut. I was
clueless and asked my father for help. He found the flat for
me - barely four miles from our old home - and apologised;
he said that if I could bear it for a year or so, I could sell it
and buy something better and be in the enviable position of

being some way up the ladder. He was surprised and gratified, I think, to see how delighted I was with what he'd found for me. I wouldn't have swapped it for my brother's whole house, or for anything. My little flat, with its freshly plastered walls and rather predictable oatmeal carpets, was quiet and warm and safe and hidden and everything I needed at that point in my life. It was my instant home. It was my cure.

I'd left university triumphant with a First but depleted with the effort of acquiring it. As I've mentioned already, I was a grafter by nature and I'd simply grafted myself out. The doctor said it was mental exhaustion and asked why I thought I had so much to prove. I remember scowling at him.

I returned home looking for sanctuary but found, instead, two people who wanted to move on and enjoy themselves and no longer have to care for their children. My brother had done his bit by settling in the North with an affable girlfriend. But I remained a physical blockage, lying on the sofa all day, fielding incessant questions about my work plans. I'd been so impatient once to get into the world of work. Now I wondered what the rush was all about.

How did I get from being the slacker on the sofa to the working woman in her immaculate little flat? The same way I seemed to do anything of note in those days. Through my aunt.

Deirdra was a phenomenon in our family, a force of nature, eternally busy with the needs of others, the one we leant on, complained to, shared news with, paid heed to, and regularly quoted. A marshaller of people. My father's elder sister – the only one of that generation of the family to go to university – was a free-thinker and a straight-talker. For years, I strove to become a version of her; she seemed so strong and quick-witted, so admirable. Deirdra was a social worker and of indeterminate politics. She had two children who appeared to be bringing themselves up, and she had what I read as a special regard for me.

Ah, I see her now, with her red curls faded to beige, her snub nose and her parchment skin (I get a lot of my looks from her). When she smiled her face seemed to crack apart, lines exploding and radiating from her eyes, nose and mouth. She held people to her as though it were her way of reading and reassuring them. To me, Deirdra was the fire in the cave I always came back to, the place of safety. I could tell her anything and asked her so many things. She was instinctively generous with her love and time and, though fearsomely busy, never balked at stopping to give genuine consideration to my many problems. She was immensely practical when it came to love and life, wasn't the type to dream about what might or might not be.

The other thing that marked her out – along with her generosity – was her astonishing news-gathering abilities. She should have been the reporter, not me. She retrieved other people's information like she was bringing the word of God down from the mountainside. Facts, tip-offs, lectures, all came back to us from nebulous sources. But dammit they always had the knack of rousing me out of my doldrums or boosting me with the enthusiasm required to get through a day.

How frustrated she must have felt at the sight of me – her true disciple, the one to carry on her good work – lying inert and idle, a drain on my family, the embodiment of gutless-ness. She came often and tried to entice me off that sofa with information about work experience or voluntary positions. I batted them away. I remember there was an arrogance about me, born of fear and misgivings. It already occurred to me at that early point that I might have shot my mouth off and that I was really a very ordinary girl with very ordinary defects.

But after several months of coming and going and cajoling and wheedling and manoeuvring, she did – all credit to her – manage to get me off the sofa and out into the world.

I remember her squatting down next to me and brushing my hair out of my eyes.

"Still nothing going on, love?" she asked.

I didn't want to speak to her, was both ashamed and aggrieved.

"You're only human," she observed and sat down properly on the carpet with her legs out in front of her, like a toddler.

"I'm just fed up with people always asking me what I'm going to do," I whined.

"I'm not surprised. But really you shouldn't give a stuff about other people's views. You must do everything in your own sweet time."

"I know," I said.

"But this is the thing," and she shuffled towards me with her buttocks. I had to smile at the sight of her and she laughed on my cue. "You don't want to fall into a big black hole, do you? You don't want to get obsessed with yourself. It's a horrible business, self-obsession. Makes a person very unhappy."

My lips were trembling.

"But how do I stop?"

My arm was hanging over the edge of the sofa and she reached for my hand and held it tightly. She was giving me permission to cry.

"Shall I tell you the secret to perfect contentment? Shall I? It's to focus as much as you can on other people. Turn your attention away from yourself and onto others. Help them. Helping people makes you happy. Makes you feel good."

"OK," I said, between my tears. "I'll try."

"That's my beautiful girl. You have such a wonderful life ahead of you. Don't fret about anything. It will all work out."

"I won't," I said, nodding, the tears dropping onto the velour of the sofa.

"You're clever, you're good and you're going to do wonderful things. Just start slowly. One little step at a time. Prove yourself. Make yourself firm and sure and then you can do anything."

I was still nodding but by now unable to contribute anything more than snot and gulps and gasps.

"Now," she said and her pretty porcine features were inches from my damp face. "Let it all out and then soon you can sit up and head out. I've got a little job for you."

"You have?"

"That's right. It's voluntary, but it's a start. Renfrew House. Heard of it?"

A nod turned halfway to a shake.

"It's a good place. Home for kids in care. In Catford. I know the warden. She and I thought it might be nice for someone to come in and help some of the older ones prepare for exams. Help get them into college and university. I know just the person for that job, I told her."

"Tutoring?" I asked.

"Yes," and she smiled so warmly that the tears came back at once. "Do something of use, my love. Help others. And just you see how quickly you help yourself."

She leant over, kissed me and struggled to her feet with a "gor blimey – don't let me go down there again!".

"Things will happen," she said, looking down at me. "Never you worry. Be patient and be ready."

And so I got up and almost at once I was planning how my lessons would go and where I could get hold of specimen exam papers and revision guides. I could hear myself encouraging reluctant learners or coaxing the half-hidden intellect out of the shy. I could do this.

Within a fortnight I was sitting in the bedroom of a fifteen-year-old girl at Renfrew House, asking her about her posters and wall art and creasing open a new exercise book in readiness for notes.

It wasn't a cataclysm. I didn't change overnight. I didn't even enjoy the intellectual side much, finding that any kind of return to education – even on behalf of others – brought with it a sense of familiar tedium, of being left behind, but Deirdra had been absolutely right: my focus shifted away from me and that felt good.

I was getting hungrier now for something more and that had only happened because I was out, sampling the wider world. I couldn't expect Deirdra to come to my aid all the time. I had to find the opportunities for myself, but I couldn't keep her away. She was as keen as I was to see me progress.

So often we came to gentle blows because she heard of an opening on some publication or another and wanted me to jump at the chance before the door closed on it. I told her over and again that I needed to be qualified, that I couldn't just walk onto a newspaper without some evidence that I knew what I was doing. And training cost money.

Before long her contacts came through for her once again. She called round one day and, as I was making us both a cup of tea, she sidled up to me in the kitchen, giggling, and pressed something into my free hand before jumping back and watching me with a hand over her mouth.

It was a cheque for eight hundred pounds.

"And now my niece gets her journalistic training. Ta-dah."

"How can you afford this?" I wanted to know, inspecting the cheque in a daze.

"I applied on your behalf for a bursary. That woman who knows that other woman who works on that magazine told me about it. It couldn't have been simpler."

"Deirdra! That's not how it works."

"Clearly it is, sweetheart."

"But it's for me to apply for bursaries."

She gave me a sour look.

"Now," she said, "don't be ungrateful. People want to help. Let them."

"What people? Who is this woman who knows a woman? And at which magazine?"

"What does it matter? I'll pass on your thanks, shall I? And the best thing you can do is to start applying for a training course."

Have the good grace to accept this, I told myself. My pride was pulsing angrily against it but it could just as well have been excitement.

"I'm going to put the money in the bank first," I told her earnestly.

"Fine."

"It'll be safe there."

"It will."

I put the money in the bank and did as she asked, and I managed to find a course in a further education college on the South Coast and applied for it. They told me I was a little more *educated* than most applicants and didn't I want to try my luck directly with a national newspaper? "No," I said primly. "I want to learn my trade as a news reporter. I want to start from the bottom and work up. I'm that kind of person. I take my time."

I take my time.

I think of that now, the little glimpses I had of my true self even then. I am excruciatingly slow at everything. I'm always the last to catch on. It's a beautiful moment when it all dawns on me at last but it takes so long. It's just the way I work.

When I completed my course and returned to London, my father greeted me by shaking me by the hand – "We knew you had it in you, love," he pronounced shyly – and presented me with the news that they'd sold the house and that I was to get a cut of the money.

And so I had a home and I found a job and that's how smoothly, ultimately, I entered the adult world and backed off from the academic, institutionalised life that had seemed to fit me so well and whose eccentric daily patterns I had still longed for in that first year of my release from them. It wasn't that hard to adapt. But these things are relatively easy when you have people on your side; dear, good people who want the best for you. If I were the type to use such language, I would have said I was blessed. But I don't believe in that kind of thing. People help you and you should be gracious enough to accept it and make the absolute most of it. And I did.

☙

Every weekday morning, I breakfasted at 7.30 in my kitchen, the radio on, the thumps of slamming doors coming from the flats downstairs. (We were all young working people in that house, all migrating into Town during the day). Then I'd head down to the station where I caught the train to Charing Cross and from there walk to the magazine publisher just off Oxford Street. I was one of eight editorial staff at *The Builder*, four of us reporters, and spent my days writing about underpinning and insulating, deadloads and party walls. I interviewed managers of aggregate suppliers and marketing directors of double-glazing companies. I talked timber, glass and brick and travelled outside the capital to take pictures of building sites and housing estates. I had a particular expertise in heating, ventilation and air-conditioning and I got on very well with the director of the Association of Plumbing and Heating Contractors. I loved every blessed (there I go again!) minute of it. I loved how my intellectual world had reduced itself to such specifics, and how my colleagues and I could get so excited about technical details that weren't native to any of us.

Often, in the evenings, I opted for the bus over the train and, being in no particular rush, would relish the slow un-folding of my journey, my head bumping sleepily against the window, the streets outside bristling with a readiness to live, with an angry and glorious demand on life. I was a micro-scopic part of it, and it seemed more than enough to me. At home I cooked for myself and ate my dinner in front of the TV and invariably bathed before bed.

At the weekends I had my interests. I'd taken up dress-making, possibly out of nostalgia for the remembered sight of my mother's own craft projects laid out in the spare room. For a special treat I'd go to the West End and the John Lewis haberdashery department, where I'd buy a new pattern and choose some fabric. Back in the flat, the furniture would be pushed against the living-room wall and the fabric and pattern pieces laid on the floor, often stretching out beyond the front door and into the narrow hallway beyond. A Saturday gone, spent cutting and pinning fabric. A Sunday whiled away with a swim at the local pool, a bit of shopping, coming home to sew, to read, to look out of the porthole at Kent.

Sometimes I'd drop in on one of my fellow residents in the house, just briefly, to say hello. Sometimes they called on me. I was particularly fond of two girls my age who shared the flat directly beneath me, one a teacher, the other a lawyer. Abi and Kate. They were the epitome of ambition and energy, a delightful pair who held parties and played the kind of music I came to realise I liked, and who took in parcels for me if I was out. When I went shopping, I'd call in to ask if they needed anything. They did the same. On a couple of occasions, they invited me round to watch a video. I remember sitting on their battered old sofa between them, glass of wine in hand, contented, nothing to worry about, nothing deeper playing on my mind than whether I'd bought the right sized buttons for the dress I was making or if I should take my work suit to the dry cleaners.

I stayed up late on Fridays, sewing or reading, and I lay in bed on Saturday mornings, unrushed, getting out to make toast and returning to eat it while planning my day. I contemplated getting a cat. A cat would be all the company I required and it would look after itself happily while I was at work. I would come home and it would vacate the bed to greet me – leaving a round space of warmth I could run my hand over. Such a small ambition – to get a cat – but, at the time, the extent of my dreams.

Once a fortnight, on a Wednesday evening, I took a different bus home via Renfrew House where I'd spend two hours with three young people, discussing exam strategies and helping them to rehearse their prepared answers.

This unremarkable existence is remarkable to me now because it ran counter to everything I had thought I would be doing by that stage of my life. Not sewing cotton lawn dresses and duvet covers, for God's sake, but attending political rallies and making my name in the Party. Not spending half an hour at a time gawping at a distant county but writing articles on poverty, inequality, the rest of it. How had I let those pressing ambitions stall? But they weren't stalled, as such. No, no. They were alive and I never for a second lost my hold on them. I just needed to recover. I needed to get my breath back. There was no rush, surely? I was young. I had so much time. I couldn't do it all, not yet. I needed to focus on settling into this kind of life. I needed time to grow into myself, into the adult me, the rational, experienced new me. The one who might be of some use to the world one day. As Deirdra had advised, I was making myself firm and sure.

I told myself that this was the time to forgive myself: that I couldn't cure all the world's ills alone and maybe nobody would notice or care too much if, for a little while at least, I plodded on with a nothing kind of life, a quiet, easy sewing-at-home, watching-videos-with-friends kind of existence. A bourgeois life.

It lasted around two years and then, fully recovered, I seemed to be inviting the world in again. I learnt that however precious those humdrum moments were to me, they could not remain as the top note, or not if I wished to progress in any way. An old life was ending. Things became more complicated. My home life changed. And my work life was about to change, too.

⁂

My aunt said she would see me in Soho Square at lunchtime. It was round the corner from my office and so it was perfectly convenient for me to meet her there. Not at all convenient for her, though. She was going to a lot of trouble and she had her reasons, as I well knew. I'd been at *The Builder* for nearly three years. Many of my colleagues had moved on and those who stayed were unlikely to go on to anything better. I loved that shabby office and the routine of my working life but as each old face was replaced by a new one, I found myself bitten by impatience.

It was a bright, cold day and workers had emerged from their offices underdressed, thinking it was Spring and that they could sit out for lunch. But the air was raw, I remember, and I'd gone back for my coat. Deirdra was on a bench, under a huge tree in new bud. She was wearing her thick tartan jacket and baggy jeans, her hair erupting from a topknot.

"Look at you!" she said, as I approached. "Dressed like an executive."

"Just my work suit," I told her. "I'm meant to be going to an industry briefing in Westminster later. Don't wear the suit every day."

"Industry briefing in Westminster," she repeated. "Listen to her."

I settled beside her on the bench and we nestled.

She grabbed one of my hands and pressed it tightly.

"You'll never guess," she grinned.

64

"You're right."

"All that waiting. Well, it had to be for something."

"Go on, just tell me. What's up?"

"I've written it all down, so don't worry about the details."

I shook my head, laughing.

But for a moment, she merely took me in, and it felt good, if a little awkward, to be loved and admired this much.

"I told you to wait, didn't I?" she said at last. "I told you to be patient."

"Deirdra, please just tell me."

And so she did.

"First thing this morning I had a call from someone who said she used to work with me in Lambeth though I'm not sure I remember her. I think I do. I think I recognised her voice. Nice quiet lady who used to work part-time. If it's her. If it *is* the one I'm thinking of, then she worked on the children's home assessments with me.

"Sorry. Wittering on. Well, how grand is this? She says she remembers how I used to go on about my niece trying to break into journalism and she'd just heard from *her* friend, who works on *The Messenger*, and who *she* barely remembers as well, that there might be an opening for you."

Just to hear the word *Messenger* produced a rush of strange sensations. My stomach slipped over and my heartrate quickened, all those responses you read about in love stories in one queasy rush.

"Have I ever mentioned this woman to you?"

She hadn't.

"I'm sure it's who I think it is. So, the thing is, they're taking on a trainee for the first time in years and they're looking for a young, qualified reporter who can start immediately. They're not advertising it because they know they'll be swamped with applicants. It's all word of mouth to begin with. She came straight to me as soon as she heard. I mean I'm just flabbergasted that people can be so nice. What do you think?"

And my mind switched itself back at last.

"Oh God, oh God. Do you think I've got a chance?"

The Messenger. A national newspaper, left-leaning, liberal, highly-respected, whose columnists I read every day, whose politics chimed with mine. This was beyond fantastical. Had she been right all along? That if you nudge yourself in roughly the right direction, you'll be ready to jump when the opportunity comes? Was this the reward for my patience?

My aunt took charge, stopped us both drifting.

"This is your big break. Don't squander it. Act right now. Just write them a letter full of passion but normal – keep it normal, don't sound desperate. And tell them everything you've done. They just want evidence that you're serious about this."

"Serious? Oh my God, I'm *so* serious."

"Good girl, now over to you."

I sensed her relax and her grip loosen. But I was going the other way, my body buzzing with euphoria and trepidation.

"I'll screw it up!" I exclaimed.

"No, you won't."

She took a piece of paper from her pocket on which was scribbled a name: *Guy Thornsbeech.* Underneath it was the postal address of *The Messenger.*

"Write to him," she said. "Do it today. Do it at the office as soon as you get back from this Westminster thing. Or before. Do it before! Put your CV in. Ask for an interview. Tell him you can make any day, any time."

"I'll muck it up. I just know I will."

"Now stop it," she said. "You and I both know that's not true. But, listen to me," and she turned my face to mirror hers. "Better not tell you-know-who."

I tried to focus, and realised she was warning me.

"Deirdra, I can't *not* tell him."

"Tell him when you've got it. Until then, it's just your business."

I was going to remonstrate or at least try and say something mildly disapproving. But she was right. If I told him now he'd almost certainly get upset and start agonising about the end of our relationship. And then I might falter. It wasn't a home thing, anyway. It was a work thing, and if I sorted it all out at work then I needn't bring it home at all.

Deirdra knew that it was dawning on me and so she nodded and patted my hand and made to get up.

"Get a wriggle on," she said and kissed me before she left me there on the bench to think about the turn of events and the reasons I should tread carefully if I wanted them to work out well.

And so I suppose I should tell you about you-know-who. It's not that I wasn't going to. It's just that I didn't quite know how to introduce him. Deirdra has done it for me.

2

IN THE EARLY summer of '93, I went with Deirdra and two of the teenage girls from the care home to take part in the anti-road protests at Oxleas Wood. I had been reading about the proposed river crossing for months and been impressed by the level of direct action trying to stop it. I exulted in the thought of ordinary people taking a stand against government. Residents were doing everything in their power to stop the huge motorway cutting through the centre of this ancient woodland and it seemed to be working. Some of them were even willing to sell their own homes to pay for a court case against the Department of Transport. I couldn't think of anything more rousing and significant than the superhuman efforts these people were making. Yes, there were national environmental organisations and all kinds of pressure groups coming in from the outside, but it was the people of Shooter's Hill and Eltham and Woolwich who earned my greatest respect. You can do it! I thought. You have it in you to change the world.

And so on a warm July evening, the four of us went to see things for ourselves and what we found was a lovely downward swathe of meadow in Greater London, peaceful, precious, and skirted by a thick band of woodland. Almost instantly you could feel its age, appreciate the staggering achievement of it simply remaining there after so much around it had been tarmacked and built over.

There were groups of people dotted around the broad grassy incline, and tents and gazebos, with slogans painted on boards and banners declaring support for the campaign. I found it heavenly, my young heart stirred by the sight of so many people coming together to change what must have seemed so unchangeable at first. That evening they were on the cusp of victory and they could sense it – the atmosphere was buoyant and positive. The two girls from the care home settled with a party of other young people and Deirdra instantly made herself known to a pair of women of exactly her cast, which meant I was free to wonder among the protesters and imbibe.

Use this, I told myself. *Remember how passionate people can be, how they can step out of their ordinary lives and do something memorable.*

I was beyond thrilled with myself. That evening on that ancient hill to the south of the Thames, as the sun staggered its way to the hazy green horizon, I was burning up with excitement. I could do anything.

Of course, I thought of her.

I felt her near me, as I so often did. I saw us pacing around her college room, laughing, stomping about like idiots, so close, entirely in tune.

Go out and do it, she had said.

"I will!" I said out loud and the sky and the trees were my witnesses. "I will. I'll do so much with my life."

"But first, will you sign this?" he asked.

I turned to find a man in black jeans and a white t-shirt with a clipboard and pen. He was amused.

"To show your solidarity for our comrades at Twyford Down."

I knew I was beautiful that night. Sounds improbable,

doesn't it? I am small and unremarkable, pale. Traditional-looking, if you like. But that evening there was something inside me that powered to get out and I know it showed on my face. There have been moments in my life – just a few – when I've been sure that I was somebody worth noticing.

I could tell he noticed me.

"This is all so wonderful," I told him as I signed the petition.

"It is, isn't it? The rumour is they'll be withdrawing the scheme any moment."

He stretched his arms out wide and breathed in the evening air.

"We've done it. We've won."

"I wish I'd been involved," I said.

"You're here. That's something."

I envied him. He could claim ownership of a great moment. I could only look on.

We parted after a few more words and he went off in search of more signatures.

Deirdra was as exhilarated as I was. When she found me, she grabbed my hand and said: "You see! I told you. There's no better feeling that to be part of something, something that's bigger than you, that benefits others."

"Do you mind if I go home alone?" I asked her. "I have this feeling that I want to hang around a bit."

She had to take the two girls back to Renfrew House and so she conceded, telling me to be careful and not to stay too late.

"Deirdra, I'm twenty-five."

"And that makes you invincible."

Yes. Yes, it did.

My plan was to walk home, all the way along Shooter's Hill and to Blackheath, Lewisham and finally back to my own house on the hill. More than six miles. It would take half the night, but it was summer and I was young and didn't want this feeling to end.

❧

He caught up with me barely five minutes into my journey.

"Mind if I join you?" he asked. "Not a good idea, a young woman walking alone round here."

I strode on.

"Sure," I said. "But it's a long walk. You might not want to hang around."

"I'm more than happy to hang around. Hanging around is my forte," he said.

And we walked on as the sun finally disappeared.

❧

That night on that long trek through the southern reaches of our city, I felt something novel: I could talk, easily, and honestly to this man. I could be funny and wise and, at moments, conversationally dominant. I had no inhibitions and was - as my mother used to say - not at all backwards about coming forwards. I was playful and then earnest and then mischievous again.

And him? Well, he was agog. He laughed a lot, kept up as well as he could, asked me many questions, seemed to marvel at things that I thought pretty commonplace: my work, my home, my many hobbies.

His name was Simon and he was two years older than me. He lectured part-time at a brand new university in East London. His subject was law – though he'd never practised – and he specialised in human rights. He was good-looking: tall and very slim, with a cap of short black wavy hair and expressive brown eyes. He had Indian and Jewish blood in him, he told me within ten minutes of our walk. This fact deeply impressed me. I mentioned my Irish roots, as though we were exchanging qualifications.

In fact, everything I ascertained about him on that walk appealed to me, even the otherwise sombre information that he was estranged from his parents and had had an unhappy childhood. On the whole, I was in love with myself that night and I think a little of that feeling coloured my impression of him and probably anyone else who might have been there.

There was no doubt that, for each one of us, the other fitted an ideal.

"You're an amazing person," he told me. "You just live life to the full. Do what you want. Enjoy yourself."

We were standing on the eastern edge of Blackheath. The sky, the grass, the roofs and the treetops, were all pink-tinged purple. Lights glimmered at the edge of our view.

"I've got plans," I told him suddenly. "Big plans."

"Me too," he said. "We've got a lot in common."

I don't know who instigated it, but we held hands.

"This is our moment. For our generation," he said. "We mustn't let it pass."

I may shudder at the inanity of it now, but at the time it was about the most monumental thing I'd ever heard.

The sewing machine was moved to make way for a computer. They were still as deep as they were tall, computers, in the mid-90s, and this monster dominated the little sewing table that I had kept against the back wall of my bedroom. This was where he would work while I went out to my job. He had multiple investigations going at the same time and his book was going to feature them all in a kind of patchwork of issues. I never really got the gist of what the book was about despite our discussing it every single day. The title kept changing and he fiddled with the idea constantly, frequently declaring himself ready to move on to actually writing it, only to collapse in despondency that it "wasn't quite right". It was angry, that much I know. He said he was *voicing the anger of the streets.*

Simon was charismatic, energetic, affectionate. Everything about him seemed delicate and sensitive; his neck, fingers, forehead, the slim sliver of a nose. He was like some ethereal figure in a pre-Raphaelite painting, slightly effeminate-looking at first sight but interestingly handsome. He tended to pull me onto his lap when he wanted to talk to me and kept me pinned there. His pet names for me were slightly sickly. There is an art to the finding the right pet name for one's lover but it wasn't something either of us could get quite right.

We had been seeing each other for around five months when he told me that his landlord was selling his bedsit and that he needed somewhere to live. Of course, it went without saying that he should move in with me. We were definitely a couple and told each other often how great we were for each other, how great we were for the world.

There was love. I can't say there wasn't. And attraction, most definitely on my side. The more vulnerable he seemed, the more I wanted to lift him up and make him feel good about himself. I was prepared to do this in bed, where I was more than ready to have adventures and finally discover a new playground, but he took sex very seriously. For him it was a silent, almost solemn affair, that should be respected and most certainly shouldn't be talked about or ridiculed. I longed to play, but in the end I took my lead from him.

We fell into a pattern of behaviour based around his needs. He needed money, which was exclusively earned by me, admiration, which would come from his book (a full-time occupation within three weeks of him moving in), and he needed me to continue being what I was: upbeat, deferential and companionable.

But what about my home, with him in it? Inevitably it changed. As soon as Simon moved in, my little flat ceased to be dear to me. It became very obviously small and confining. I couldn't be alone anywhere, couldn't experience silence and indolence. And if I needed to escape it, to go for a walk, then he came with me and brought the confinement right along with us. I didn't want to call on Abi and Kate downstairs if it meant taking Simon with me. They stopped calling on me, after a few occasions of having the door opened to them by a sullen boy-man who failed to greet them or ask them in.

The place was suddenly full of things. His books were stacked against all the walls and he brought no fewer than three guitars with him. I never resented him for it – people own things, it's not a crime – but I couldn't quite relax in my own habitat, my eyes always coming to rest on something in the middle of the floor or the eternally full washing basket or the shopping still on the kitchen counter hours after it had been bought by him in the morning. No, I must repeat, none of this is a crime. None of this matters – and I understand that so keenly now – if you have reached a place of glad sacrifice. It's just washing, just cans of beans. They don't matter. Flesh and blood matter. Love matters.

I mattered – deeply – to him.

"We've sussed it, haven't we, little chicky-girl. We've got it just right," he told me. "You love your job, I love mine. It's all coming together. The future is gonna be beautiful. The world needs people like us."

The future didn't involve marriage (a "vile institution") or children ("it's a criminal act against the planet to make more humans") and so he was proposing him and me for the rest of our days. I preferred not to think about the rest of our days just then, often wriggled out of the discussions when they were dropped on me from nowhere.

So why did Deirdra feel unable to come to my flat to talk to me there? She never came to the flat, had had one too many heated arguments with Simon, whose politics were way to the left of hers and who never gave way on any points.

Why did she ask me not to tell him about the prospective job interview at *The Messenger*? We both knew why. Because there was an understanding that he was in line for the first piece of success, not me, and that if something good happened to me then it would upset the balance.

The older sister always marries first. And if the younger one does, then the older one is totally done for and will wither away unnoticed. Isn't that in the Bible or something? There is an order to things, and I wasn't meant to be the next in the queue.

3

I'D ONLY HAD one other job interview in my life – and that's surprising in itself – but even I knew that the one for the trainee reporter post on *The Messenger* was a little unconventional.

I brought cuttings with me and two references, but Guy Thornsbeech, who was the news editor and conducting the interview, accepted them without enthusiasm and muttered that he'd inspect them later. He was not an empathetic kind of soul; there was something bloodless and businesslike about him. He was around fifty at the time, very fit, with a film of silver hair.

"We want someone who is hungry for the job and who is happy to graft," he explained.

His choice of words instantly caught a flame under my bubbling excitement.

"That's me!" I exclaimed. "This would mean everything to me. I know my job at the moment isn't very glamorous but it proves, I hope, that I'm serious about my aims."

"And what are your aims?"

And so out came an adapted version of the life plan. I explained my interest in politics while stressing my political neutrality, which both he and I knew to be laughably off the mark but somehow necessary. I told him that my dream was to work my way up to home affairs correspondent or something political – however long it took. But I wanted to learn my craft, I said, and I wanted to learn it on the only national newspaper that counted, the only honest, free-thinking, genuinely influential one. That's what I said and that's how I said it: with breathless respect.

He nodded and said: "All right".

That was more or less it. We shook hands and I got up.

"Would you like a quick look at the newsroom?" he suggested.

I told him I very much would.

We left the conference room where the interview had just taken place and stepped into the corridor. Almost immediately the door to another large meeting room opened and a party of suited men came out.

As if a light had been switched on or a window opened, the atmosphere changed at once. These men were different to the ones I had so far worked with, looked and sounded different, and they brought a different air with them. They were confident, loud, each trying to talk above the other. They took up the corridor at once, like a flood filling a channel, so that Guy and I had to step back and press ourselves against the wall to let them out. I glanced up at the animated faces as they passed. Several glanced down at me, checking me out, just in case I was worth a second look. I watched this vigorous masculine mass move on and as they did so, one of them, a tall, lean young man with blond hair, turned to look directly at me. I thought he was going to say something and kept my eyes on his. They were a pale denim blue, those eyes, and a little terrified – particularly as they met mine – like he'd been caught out looking at me. He was around my age and there was, therefore, an instant of recognition and mutual interest. I find beautiful male faces arresting. But that was that. A moment.

When they had vacated the corridor, leaving behind them echoes of their laughter and a whiff of their genial bastardy, I looked to Guy Thornsbeech for an explanation. He sighed.

"Shareholder meeting. Not a journalist among them and yet they make the decisions. Say what you like – it's all money and influence."

I gave him a consolatory half-smile but he had already turned his back and was heading towards a set of double doors. When we reached them, he stepped back, pushed one open and let me go ahead.

The minute I walked into that huge, humming, pleasantly reverberating space, I was overwhelmed with the compulsion to become a part of it. It felt like the most glorious factory in the world, busily producing – oh God, did I really think this? – the truth. The facts. The stories that reflected the state of our society and called out its inequalities and irregularities. It all started here, in this satisfactorily aloof club of genteel mill workers. They sat at their desks – two to each and opposite each other – in various poses of engrossment, the atmosphere surprisingly muted, chatter so low-level that you could have fallen asleep to it, occasional stifled laughter, the hypnotic tap of the keyboard alongside the soothing thrum of rain against the long bank of windows running along one side of the room. For someone who didn't much care what she wore, I yearned to look like the few women I saw, in their stripes and scarves. And the men? Now that's what I felt men should look like: no ties, no suits. Brains.

Oh, let me work here! Please, please. It was as if all that ambition – all the passionate hopes I had unpacked for her that summer night in that little cell of a room – were suddenly back on the conveyor belt and travelling in the right direction.

I can make a mark. I can be of greater use. Just you see.

I felt a tap on the shoulder and looked around to find Guy holding the door open.

I slipped out and stopped beside him in the corridor, thanking him and trying to move off politely, now that the interview and the tour were over. My stomach was in a knot of fear. To have seen this and then to lose it would be beyond agony.

"Listen," he said, and he followed it with a long silence as he stroked his chin and chewed over his words.

"Yes?" I asked.

"Well, it's like this. You can have it."

"I'm sorry?"

"The job. I mean, the traineeship. You're just right for it. I knew from the start."

"I don't understand," I told him. I didn't. This wasn't how these things worked. There was always keen competition and at least some kind of discussion between the bosses. A person was always made to wait. It was part of the process.

"I run the newsroom," he said, almost as though he had divined my doubts. "You're in."

I gaped at him. He smiled in return. A kind of smile, anyway.

"There are the usual formalities. Something to sign. It'll be sorted by personnel. Sorry, human resources."

And still I couldn't move. So *he* did. He left me there in that corridor, waiting for something more, something that might explain what had just happened.

I left that building in a daze and stood in the rain and didn't want to go home or to *The Builder* offices and so I walked around the City, stopping at a small overly heated café where the steam was so pervasive it felt like entering a rainforest. The coffee machine spluttered, the solicitors and the bankers all came and then went with their coffee.

I've done it. I've only bloody gone and done it, I told myself. Or her. I think I was speaking to her.

I've arrived.

༺༻

Four weeks later I was sitting at my own desk in *The Messenger*'s newsroom, dressed in my new white shirt and new black 501s and accepting the sober congratulations of my new colleagues on my appointment. The first day was made up of verbal back-slapping and a lot of requests after my general comfort and happiness. I lost count of the number of times my fellow journalists suggested that I should simply ask them if I needed anything or wanted to know where anywhere was.

I didn't dare, of course. I didn't dare do anything, least of all bother Guy with any suggestion that I might do some work. It would all happen in its own sweet time, I told myself. In the meantime, I could think about getting a nice trouser suit, plain black or brown, in readiness for assignments. And some shoes, something with a bit of a heel. Maybe I needed a hair cut . . .

By the end of the second day, the worries had set it. Was I meant to be approaching the news desk with my story ideas? Should I remind them that I was there? The news desk was comprised of four senior journalists, all male, led by Guy, who left at six every day to be replaced by the night news editor and his team. Behind them and making up a good third of the room sat a bank of sub-editors constantly at their screens, rarely getting up, set apart from the reporters and also all male.

At the end of the week nothing had changed. Nobody was offering me any help anymore, nobody was congratulating me. Everyone was busy and nobody wanted to be bothered. I had achieved nothing but sat and looked at the clock and experienced pure, perfect, boredom.

That Friday I went home and in a tragic tone told Simon that he had been right.

When I had originally told him about the interview and job offer at *The Messenger*, it looked as if he might cry. He went to his computer screen and stared at it for an hour. Over dinner he said portentously: "This is the beginning of the end."

"Don't be ridiculous."

"You'll meet someone else."

"Rubbish."

He reached across the kitchen table and held my hand.

"Can't you wait until I get my book published and then go off and get your kicks?"

I pulled my hand away.

"I'm not *going off to to get my kicks*. I'm just changing jobs.

His tears were beginning for real.

"I'm a failure, aren't I? I'm never going to achieve anything."

I hadn't been expecting that level of disintegration. I went and sat on his lap at once and kissed him and told him everything was going to be fine.

"You'll work longer hours," he muttered. "I like you in the house with me while I'm working. It helps me write. It helps me to know you're there. I won't be able to do anything now. And you can forget Renfrew House. You won't have time for your good deeds."

"I'll do it at the weekend."

"Oh, so I'll see even less of you. What about me? What am I supposed to do?"

"You'll be fine," I said. "You're just a bit caught out by the speed of things. I understand. So am I. But Si, I couldn't be happier. This is my dream job. This means I'm on my way."

His rather touching defencelessness, which had so affected me, evaporated at once and something more intransigent pushed through.

"You'll hate it," he said coldly and pushed me off his lap.

And now here I was, barely a few weeks after that conversation, throwing his prophesy right back at him, as though he should have stopped me, as though I'd been thrown to the wolves with his blessing. This time I was the one on the verge of tears.

"Just resign. Who cares?" he told me casually. "I *said* you weren't cut out for that kind of life."

I was already so lost that I didn't have anything to cling on to but his words.

He was at his desk, my old sewing table, and had pushed his glasses up on his head.

"You must know it," he said. "You're too nice to work on a national newspaper or to go into politics. People like you don't have it in them. It's nothing to be ashamed of, little chicky. Better you find out now. Forget it for today and put in your resignation at the end of the month."

"I'm not sure," I said quietly, confronted for the first time by a fear that had always been there inside me.

"It's just not you, sweetie," he said and his glasses dropped back down onto his nose and he turned back to the screen. "You must have known."

4

"RIGHT. I SUPPOSE you'd better come over to my desk for this."

God knows how long he had been standing there. And God knows who he was. I'd never seen him before. But there he stood, his sleeves pushed up, a fearsome frown on his face, giving off a sense of outrage at having to speak to me at all.

I didn't know what to say, so I shook my head.

This incensed him further. *Idiot woman – can't even express herself.*

But the outrage wasn't merely reserved for me.

"Oh, for fuck's sake. Didn't they tell you?" he fumed.

"No," I said, hoping this would win me some sympathy and an explanation.

He sighed vastly.

"I'm supposed to be mentoring you. I'm Jay. Like the bird, not the initial. Jay Corey. You're to come over to the subs' desks and see what we do."

"Am I?"

"Apparently it's all part of your traineeship. But why me? Why not the chief sub? I'll tell you why, shall I? Because he's too busy and clearly I'm not."

He was already moving away and I was getting up and following him.

We weaved through the reporters' desks – hands typing, hands reaching for phones, hands making notes – skirted the news desk and arrived in that strange land I'd never yet had cause to visit: the subs' desks. He occupied his chair and I stood behind him and stared down at the top of his head while he grunted details about the software *The Messenger* used and how pages were set and everything else that held zero interest for me. He pulled up some recently filed copy from a foreign correspondent.

"This is the rubbish I deal with on a daily basis. A thousand literals, a total dearth of story-writing skill."

I inspected the screen and saw a stolid block of words. It looked nothing like airy newsprint.

"That's from one of our correspondents?"

"Yes. I don't know why we employ him."

Why are you so angry? I wondered.

I looked back down at his head and was surprised to see no parting, only a close-shaved forest of brown spikes.

"You'll do me a massive favour by giving me cleaner copy than this."

The blood vessels at his temples rippled. I saw a cut on his cheek, imagined his bitter tussle with the razor in the morning. I wondered who stroked that cheek, if anyone. Poor cow.

He talked some more about the art of the sub-editor while I followed minute trails through his scalp, and then he pushed his chair back sharply and looked up at me.

"Got all that?"

"Yes, I think so. Thank you very much."

"You're not very . . ."

"What am I not very?"

"Confident? Is that the word?"

"Funny, I was just thinking the opposite about you."

He considered this for a moment.

"It's busy today," he explained.

84

"And you're stressed."

"That's right. Because I'm – "

"Because you're stuck with a trainee."

"It's not my job to mentor people."

"I can see that. Well, I'm sorry. I shall return to my desk."

And I turned.

"Wait," he said.

I waited.

"Nothing."

⁂

I didn't resign, though I wrote the letter several times in my head. I didn't do it because I didn't have the guts and because it seemed such an ungrateful thing to do. But I knew I wasn't much of an asset for *The Messenger* and no one appeared to have any time to devote to me. I had come from a small outfit where we spent much of the day talking and now I was in a huge outfit where nobody seemed to talk to anyone else – or certainly not to me. How curious, I thought, that they had created a traineeship and yet I was supposed to pick it all up by observation or osmosis. No pointers, no instructions, no guidance at all.

As time went on, I shrank, hid behind my screen and trembled when the editor stalked past. I pretended to work and at news meetings I contributed next to nothing. As a result, people came to expect nothing from me.

There were mostly men in the newsroom in those days, graduates like me from very good universities, men who had arrived bookish and idealistic and who had to re-invent themselves in an effort to seem like hard-nosed reporters. Next to

85

none of them had come from reporting jobs outside London or reporting jobs full stop. *The Messenger,* for some aloof reason, recruited its daily reporting staff from the intelligentsia of the Left – researchers and post-graduates who knew their subjects inside out but had no idea how to write a news story in less than a thousand words. They spoke to their contacts, regurgitated the secrets they were told and then the subs, Jay among them, knocked their words into shape and crafted readable news stories out of them.

I was a young woman in a room full of older men who got on fine with each other and were courteous to me but considered me extraneous. The few women reporters seemed to me hell bent on making their names and were cold in a way that took me by surprise. There was no such thing as befriending among the women.

The ideas I brought to the news desk were weak and what they deemed provincial. Time after time I was knocked back with an impatient shake of the head and returned to my desk with the knowledge that, yet again, my byline would not appear in the following morning's issue.

In my first month, all I managed to produce were two half-cooked stories that I'd secretly lifted from a business paper, and which were spiked, and a page of output stats that the economics editor asked me to collate for a North Versus South industry feature. Often, in that stale and listless period, I thought back to my days at *The Builder* with the kind of nostalgia reserved for a golden childhood. I remembered the reporter I used to be: keen, engaging and full of energy. Now I was sapped and empty.

One early afternoon, while I was furtively scanning the job ads in the *UK Press Gazette,* I got called to the editor's office.

We'd never spoken at length. His name was Geoff Mattison.

"So, how do you think it's going?" he asked me.

He seemed benign enough, not in the state of near-rage that he always appeared to be as he stalked among the reporters' desks each morning. Small and with an austere, puritanical set to his features, he was almost impossible to read.

"It's all right," I tried.

He raised both brows.

"Is it?"

I shook my head.

"I'm not very good," I told him.

"You've got that right," he said.

Was I being let go? God, was this the sacking that I'd been anticipating for days now? Let's just get it over with and let me hobble away from this to something more suited to my withered confidence. Just days ago I had planned my resignation and now, faced with expulsion, I would give anything to stay.

But Mattison seemed to relent almost at once. He looked away and chewed on the lid of his pen. I waited with my mouth open, my heart on hold. When he looked back, I saw in his face the most curious mix of pity and contempt.

"It's our fault. We've let you down."

I was astonished.

"Have you?"

"It's a traineeship and we're not training you. We'll put that right."

I still didn't understand. He seemed to be apologising.

"Oh," I managed.

"Guy should be on top of this – the news editor should be keeping an eye on you, not letting you flounder alone. I'll sort it out. A trainee is an investment and the responsibility is ours. But you'd better step out of the shadows and do something soon or people will ask why you're here and someone else isn't. Someone more dynamic."

His words were immensely painful to me. To be considered a lightweight and someone undynamic, possibly taking the place of a more valuable reporter, filled me with shame. I couldn't speak to him. I was also deeply confused. I wasn't being chastised but, instead, advised. As though these things were out of his hands.

"Just put your hours in," he said. "That's all it takes. And show some curiosity. We're buying into all kinds of new-fangled databases. The world is on the verge of an information revolution – or that's what we keep telling people. You're young. Get on top of it. Right, you can go."

And that was it, the turnaround. Was it my fault, then, or theirs? If boots straps were being pulled up, shouldn't they be mine? Anyway, why wasn't I being told off? That's almost certainly what I needed and what was expected of him in this situation. I felt, perhaps, this was how *The Messsenger* differed from other newspapers: the people were decent, not the usual Fleet Street ogres, and refused to run a paper on the basis of sanctions and abuse.

I went straight to Jay's desk after the meeting.

"Hello?" he said, looking up. "Been sacked?"

"Ha-ha."

"You mean you haven't?"

"Why are you even asking?"

"Because you've just come back from Mattison's room and you're white as a sheet."

There was something so aggravating about this man. How

dare he look inside me this way? Why did he have to mock me? Simon never mocked me. And why did I feel compelled to tell him everything anyway?

"No, I haven't been sacked. In fact, he apologised for not giving me enough work."

"Right."

"Oh, so you don't believe me?"

"The editor of a British broadsheet newspaper just apologised to you? I see."

He sat back and put his hands behind his head and grinned at me.

"Oh, fuck off," I said.

"Ooooooh."

He seemed to like it when I swore.

"I said fuck off." I was beginning to crack. And so was he. The smile was elbowing its way out.

"Um, I *work* here. *You* fuck off."

A moment. Then he laughed. I laughed – eventually.

"I don't think I'm particularly liked," I heard myself confessing.

He gave this some thought.

"Listen, you want some advice?

"No!"

That smile. *What can you do with her!*

"All I was going to say was that you have to play the game. Go out to the pub with them after work. Laugh at their jokes. Buy a round."

"Do I have to?"

"If I can force myself then so can you. Just keep drinking and nodding. And when I say 'now', laugh."

I gave him an excessive scowl. I'd recently had my hair

cut very short and Jay said I looked like an angry Victorian newspaper boy. I was happily in character.

"So, you'll come too?" I asked, indifferently.

"Don't worry," he said, turning on his chair to return to his screen. "I'll be there to hold your hand."

"Tonight?"

"Tonight."

At my desk, alone at the back of the newsroom, hidden and with time on my hands, I mulled over the editor's words.

But the mulling was going in the wrong direction. You get a jolt, a kick, like something electric. It makes you sit up and shudder and look around and see things differently.

Show some curiosity, he said.

All that information. A revolution.

Just like that. Without a second thought. *I wonder what . . .*

Really? It takes someone's words to shake you and wake you? There's just no knowing when my strange, dawdling mind will catch on something. It needs inspiration. It's an entirely arbitrary and recalcitrant thing. My worst enemy.

I picked up the phone to *The Messenger's* in-house library. The old guy called Francis answered the phone.

"Can you look something up for me?" I asked him.

"On an investigation, are we?"

"Have you got lists of serving army officers?"

"The MOD has, yes. Who do you want to find?"

Just like that. Now, when I should be saving my career. Now, I want to find her. And by wanting to find her, I feel she is close. And that makes me very, very happy for one fleeting moment. I wish I knew who to thank.

"All I know is that he's an officer and he's based up North and that he's called Gartner."

"Shouldn't be a problem," said the librarian. "Is it urgent?"

Was it urgent, I thought to myself.

Go on. Why not?

"Yes," I told him. "I think it is."

⁂

The evening hand-over was taking place.

I remained at my desk at the back of the office and felt the gradual relaxation of the atmosphere. The tension of the day was dissipating. I could see Jay. He was standing at the news desk, among the departing and the arriving editors. He had a print-out in his hands and was running down a list with the night news editor. As ever, his sleeves were rolled up and I could see the dark shadow of the hair on his arms from all the way across the room.

At one point he glanced up from the sheet of paper and his eyes searched for me. I produced a tiny desk-level wave and he smiled back.

That's a lovely smile, I thought. *It transforms your face.*

Guy was getting up from his chair. I could hear laughter and goodbyes. I was never normally here by this point and was fascinated by what was clearly an important ritual. A couple of other reporters were slowly getting up and making their way to the news desk. Coats were being pulled on. Phones were largely silent. Most of the desks empty.

And then the nod from Jay. I got up and made my way across the newsroom to the gathering of men and stood at its perimeter. I had my jacket on and was holding my bag in front of me.

"Mind if our new reporter joins us?" Jay said.

Every single man turned to look at me. To look down at me.

Guy said: "Of course. More than welcome."

Only it didn't sound very welcoming. They didn't know what to make of me – I know that now – and for all their bluster and loudness, they were unsure about how to address a young woman, let alone converse with her.

As we all set off, the night news editor called after us:

"Guy, there's a story on the wires about Kenyon-Carpenter going bust."

I heard Geoff say to his mates:

"Who the fuck are Kenyon-Carpenter?"

Without a second thought and at painful length, I said: "Aggregates company. Based in the West Country. Family business. Was hoping to become a subsidiary of Dawsons and save its skin. Clearly didn't. Shame. Around 100 people will be out of work now."

Just the hint of a pause from the assembled men. Just the slightest moment to digest what had just happened.

"Good girl," said Guy and we moved off as one.

❧

In the pub, true to his word, Jay signalled and I laughed and it wasn't exactly comfortable for me, but not an ordeal either. I was on the edge of the conversation all the time, not blocked from it, but not asked in either.

I think back now and my heart is warmed by the memory

of those men. Yes, it truly is – even if I fumed about them at the time - because they were incapable of addressing me, let alone looking me in the eye, and were almost certainly feeling awkward in my company, a little less able to loosen up. I find it amusing now to think that such a socially-conscious, anti-establishment paper, that employed such patrician reporters, should have been run by a coterie of old-fashioned hacks. They took the copy of their well-mannered bookish writers and turned it into proper newsprint. None of us knew it, but they were on their way out anyway, members of an increasingly unpalatable club. Jay and I were a good 20 years younger than Guy but might as well have been from another era.

That night, Jay and I were the last to go.

The post-work crowd started thinning at around nine and we saw an empty table in the corner and leapt for it.

I bought him a drink and we settled down for another half hour of easy small talk. Nothing personal. Nothing at all awkward. Football, a bit of politics, films we'd recently seen.

Who did he have to go home to, I wondered?

We both ended it, I sensed, a little reluctantly. The table in the corner was half-hidden and the angle of the seating gave us a friendly proximity to each other which allowed us to chatter on happily without feeling too close or compromised. The hum of conversation around us was like a gentle barrier keeping us in.

"Thank you," I told him as we left. "I appreciate what you did for me tonight."

That smile again. It was the outward sign of what I suddenly realised was a most generous soul.

※

Simon was sitting on the stairs outside the front door of the flat.

"Oh no! Have you forgotten your keys?" I asked him.

"Where have you been?"

His voice was quiet but in the controlled sense.

"I told you, I was going to go out with the senior staff tonight. Jay said it would make sense. Why are you out here, Si?"

"Isn't it obvious: I'm waiting for you. Jay who?"

I opened the door and stepped into my flat.

"I've told you already. He's that arsy colleague of mine, the one who's mentoring me. I'm just trying to get on."

He didn't come in until much later. By then I'd eaten something and changed. I wasn't going to play any kind of game with him.

I went straight to bed and felt him get in later. I didn't even look at him when he pulled me to him. I didn't want him and I didn't want what followed. I imagine that was entirely the appeal.

5

OUTSIDE WORK, ONE of the only things that was truly mine by now was my fortnightly visit to Renfrew House to chat with the older teenage residents and get them exam-fit and university-ready.

One of my favourites was an eighteen-year-old girl called Avril. She was mature and sensible and not at all hesitant or self-conscious. She'd ended up in care because her grandmother, who was originally from Jamaica, had been her sole guardian and had died when Avril was only eleven. There was no extended family and the system had taken her in.

In that turbulent and troubled time in my life, Avril's easy company and immense good sense were my shelter. I made my fortnightly Renfrew routine a weekly one, just so that I could escape into her companionship more often.

She had plans, as I'd had at her age, but unlike me she was practical and realistic. She wanted to make money, to buy a home and to enjoy the benefits of her education. A career in law would give her what she calculated would be a stable and intellectually challenging life. My job was to help steer her through her sociology A level, but in reality, we just talked around her revision schedule before moving on to relevant current affairs topics.

"I'll miss you when you go away," I told her, one evening shortly before her final exams. She had, by then, a conditional offer to a very good university and there was no reason to think she wouldn't get the grades.

"Aw," she said. "We'll keep in touch. I'll be back soon. I'm a Londoner, aren't I?"

We opened that morning's papers and landed on the stories that seemed of social interest. If I remember correctly, one was about abortion being legalised in Guernsey.

"You thinking of starting a family?" she asked, shortly after our discussion.

I squirmed at the question. She had every right to ask it. At that moment I felt truly empty, with nothing of spiritual value to offer this young woman. I could have talked about journalism all evening to her. But to open my heart about something that personal appalled me.

"No," I told her. When what I meant was: I didn't want to talk about it.

"I want kids," she said. "And even if I didn't, I'd probably have them. There's only so much you can plan, right?"

I am my plan. It is part of me. No, all of me! It's a dream I'm never meant to wake up from.

"I didn't think I wanted too much," I told her in a bit of a daze. "I thought it was do-able. I had this moment when everything was clear to me and beautiful. It will come back, won't it?"

She must have wondered what I was talking about. She didn't show it.

She was ten years younger than me – poised exactly where I had been, ready to launch. I could have told her exactly what she was feeling.

I told her about the aspirations that had taken me to university and way beyond. Bit by uncompromising bit the blueprint was unfurled. Once again, I begged to know: "I will do it, won't I?"

"It's cool," she reassured me. "Course you will. But it's not like you wanna do a bungee jump or something. You know, this is long term. It's not gonna go away but you might need to let go a bit and see what happens."

"If I let go, I fail."

"No, you won't. You wanna know why?"

I did.

"Because you're a good person. Good things happen to good people."

A simple equation, and utterly meaningless. It didn't happen like that.

We pored over the paper and picked out more stories of interest and relevance to her courses.

"Do you all use computers?" she asked with a new eagerness. "In your office?"

I told her that we did. That we were on a network built specifically for *The Messenger* and which connected all the staff and meant we could file our copy directly to editors and subs.

"And are you on the World Wide Web?" she asked.

We were about to get individual access, I said.

"Wow," she said. "It's all going to be so different soon, isn't it?"

"Is it?"

"Well, just think about it," she mused. "Information coming at us from everywhere and all on a screen. Can you imagine it! Anyone can say what they want and everyone can have access to it. It changes everything."

"It changes nothing," I told her. "People will still want their information to come from verified sources. Trained reporters. Proper newspapers. I wouldn't trust anything else."

"OK," she said affably, and we continued scouring.

"I know him!" she said and her finger landed on a picture of a man I, too, dimly recognised though I couldn't quite recall why.

"Gerald French," she told me. "What's the word? Philanthropist. Very, very rich. Education, children, that kind of thing."

Of course. We interviewed him now and again. He was very outspoken about the government and their education policy at the time. His views were what they called colourful and he always had time for the media, regardless of the issue.

Avril looked up from the paper and fixed her gaze on me instead. Her clear brown eyes were strong and unwavering.

"I'd speak to his son if I were you," she told me. "He's not a happy bunny."

I was mildly intrigued but by then had already lost count of the times people had told me there was a story where there palpably wasn't. Everyone thought they knew how to do my job.

It never occurred to me to ask Avril what she knew or how she knew it.

But she was insistent.

"Just call him and ask him for his thoughts on how the Gerald French Education Trust spends its money."

That's all she would say and I told her that things didn't work like that, that I couldn't just call people on the off-chance and ask them their views.

"OK," she said. "No sweat. I've done my bit."

We read and talked more and then wandered into the

communal kitchen and made sandwiches and visited a couple of the other residents that I tutored, and I spun out the visit as long as I could because I didn't want to go home and talk to Simon. There was awfulness to come between us and I couldn't avoid it for much longer, but I couldn't face it that night either and much preferred the uncomplicated company of these wonderful young people to the inevitable craziness at home.

6

GUY SAW TO it that I was put on the Kenyon-Carpenter bankruptcy story. I was to help the business editor with research but in fact I more or less wrote the piece myself. It felt good to be on firmer ground with a subject that I knew about and could bring some authority to.

But once the story was out – under a joint byline – things returned to the usual scramble for attention. I did as the editor, Geoff Mattison, told me and hung around longer than my hours. This was not such a hardship because by now I was a regular in the pub after work.

I told Simon that my hours were increasing and that I would be coming home later and that he wasn't to worry about it or read anything into it.

In that period, my relationship with Simon was a curiosity. When he was strange and uncommunicative, I dreamt of getting away from him. When he was loving and playful, I felt something reignite between us, a possibility of something like love. It was a constant up and down. He insisted that I lay on the bed and read while he wrote, said I was his muse and that he felt comforted by my presence. I didn't grasp how I could inspire a book about urban revolt but was pleased there was such a simple way of making him extremely happy.

Of course he liked my company – he was alone at home all day. I'd loved being there myself once, looking out of the bedroom window, secure and at peace. Was there any of that left for me, I wondered, that sense of sanctuary? It didn't feel like it.

My new hideout was the corner table in the pub with Jay once all our colleagues had gone.

⁂

Jay Corey married relatively young. They met at university and for both of them it was their first great love. Getting married seemed like a wonderful, mad, brilliant, counter-intuitive thing to do. Both regretted it as soon as it was done, though neither said as much. They separated within a year. She was in marketing somewhere in the West End and they met occasionally, but there was nothing of that meteoric love still glowing in their respective universes.

This information was delivered in an entirely neutral way, as a series of facts, not as a statement of veiled intent. Jay knew about Simon anyway. To have a boyfriend reduces another party's interest in you. To have a live-in partner puts you out of reach.

And to know this and to know that Jay knew and respected this, floored me for some reason I still didn't care to examine, and gave me a taste of hopelessness.

⁂

"He's retired, your Colonel Gartner."

Francis, the librarian, left me a phone message and I went down to see him in person. There was something much more cordial and less exposed about the library and I'd find any excuse to visit it. Francis stood behind a counter, which

101

separated us from his habitat of bookcases and screens.

"Oh," I said. "Is that a problem?"

"Not for me," he replied, turning to remove a book from a shelf. "Based in Albermarle, Northumberland. Retired 1990."

"Does he have a family?"

He was already leafing through *Who's Who* for that year.

"So, Jeremy George Gartner, Royal Artillery, served briefly in Germany . . ."

"Family?"

He ran his finger along the entry.

"Wife, Yvonne, children, Douglas, Kimberley, Craig and Danielle."

There you are. Safe in your family. The baby at the end. Do I keep you there?

"I don't suppose there's a way of finding out where he lives now, is there?"

"That's your job, not mine," he said. "They're not the most common of names so you should be able to find something."

"Is it wrong?" I asked, suddenly.

"If the information is public, then I don't see why it should be."

It's not that, I wanted to tell him. *It's the violation. She's already with me so why do I need to know?*

I couldn't expect him to understand that the thought of unearthing her was repellent, was an infraction of that unspoken agreement between us, that our time together was one single night.

And would I have to literally unearth her?

The conflict must have been evident on my face. As I left he called after me. He said he would do his best to help.

Aaron French had a small voice, stung with suspicion, and questions hovered in the air between us when I told him where I was from, but for all that he didn't put the phone down on me.

I didn't even know what to ask him. I panicked when another day of non-achievement stretched before me and managed to track him down through a former employer. He was in his late twenties, well-spoken but aloof. I knew that he wasn't naturally arrogant or secretive – he was shy.

I asked him if he fancied giving me an interview as the son of a famous businessman and benefactor, that it would go towards a profile piece of his father, Gerald French.

He said no at once.

And that was pretty much all I had in my arsenal.

I filled the silence with apologies and by giving him my name and number before we rang off.

꧁꧂

He *did* want to talk to me, as it turned out, but not without giving it time and thought. When he got back to me – which took me by surprise – he was brief and clipped.

"We don't get on, my father and I," he said on our next call. I caught the formality of "father" and wondered if he ever referred more affectionately to his "dad".

I commiserated with him and assumed that we'd already reached the end of our road.

"He doesn't approve of me," he went on. "He thinks I'm a freak. Unnatural urges, that kind of thing."

I couldn't really comment. All I could do was sound neutrally sympathetic, which I was.

"I suppose you think he's very good," he said.

"I . . . I don't know. I guess so."

A long pause.

Say it. Say it.

"Gives money to charity and everything."

"He does."

Go on. Please.

"In private he's not nice at all. A total Nazi. Controlling."

Poor bloke, I thought. I understood exactly what he was saying. His dad didn't like gay people. I felt sorry for him and I felt even sorrier for myself, because a rich man not being happy with his son's sexual persuasion is not, of itself, a story.

✿

Once or twice a week I hung back and joined the others in the pub. I stood to the side of the crowd and occasionally got the joke. I was often bored.

And then they would go, and Jay and I would be left behind, waiting for our table to come free.

We'd covered a lot of conversational ground by now and what remained was the untold and untellable. For me, it was the serious doubts of my relationship with Simon. For Jay, who knows? He was recently single, as far as I knew, and lived in a flat in North London he co-owned with his brother. He seemed satisfied with his lot, when we sat together in that corner. He was very funny and looked on contentedly when I laughed.

And what did I feel? Increasingly, desire. There was a

longing growing in me, a bodily thing, a need to be pulled by him to him, to be a part of him. It was not in the slightest cerebral as it had been with Simon. The skin and hair on his arms excited me. The tiny lines at his eyes. His knuckles. His feet!

There was a strength at his very core that, to put it bluntly, did it for me.

I wouldn't have dared do anything to signal to him how I felt. It had to be my secret. But what I learnt was that there is a deep abyssal melancholy that comes with not being able to satisfy such a physical longing. To leave him each evening was, suddenly, to leave my real home.

⁂

I was due to have a "career catch-up" with Guy.

"Will it be the end of the world if I get kicked out on my arse?" I asked my aunt.

"Be strong," she said. "Be confident."

Just words. *How can I be what I'm not?*

"Everyone is rooting for you."

I wished I hadn't said anything to her at all.

⁂

"Stay with me while I write, tiny chicky. I need you."

And so I lay on the bed and I watched the back of that dark, clever head as it bobbed up and down while he wrote. His movements told me everything that he was consigning to the screen, the arguments that were even then raging inside him.

And at the end he turned around to me, beaming.

"See, you're the best. I haven't written that well in weeks. No wonder I love you so much."

⁂

"I've found the daughter," said Francis.

I looked up to see him standing over my desk.

"The daughter?" I repeated. The daughter. I sat up. My mouth was dry and I couldn't for the moment form any further words.

He placed a post-it on my desk with a flourish.

"Still using her maiden name. Still living up North. Wasn't hard."

I twisted the note round so that I could see it. It was a phone number.

Once again I looked up to him for clarification.

He had a mischievous light in his eyes, our librarian. Everything had to be a cliff-hanger for him, every discovery a peak.

"Danielle," I murmured.

He was overjoyed to be putting me right.

"What? No, the other one. Kimberley." He tapped his nose. "And now over to you."

"It'll have to wait," I told him. "I'm on to something else at the moment. Something I've been working on for a while. Got potential."

He rubbed his hands, like I was proferring a roast dinner.

"Go get 'em, young lady," he said.

⁂

Somewhere to the west of London, just beyond the Green Belt, is a care home for young people who cannot quite bring themselves to function happily in wider society. They are far from being trouble-makers or a danger to anyone. These are perfectly decent young individuals, often from comfortable backgrounds, who are bright and have excellent prospects, on paper, anyway. But they are deeply unhappy and find each day an ordeal. Their exasperated parents pay good money to this home to give their children - too old to be coddled and held - a fresh perspective and a hearty environment of brisk country walks and communal cooking and empowering discussion groups. This enlightened place - called Yew Lodge - is where these lost souls come when they are in need of bucking up. Everyone needs bucking up at some point and Yew Lodge has become the last word in it.

The home, with its pale pink walls and bean bags and gaming consoles, takes both paying residents and young people backed by charitable funds. It repays this honour by being very good at what it does. Run by a former monk, now layman, the place is simple and friendly and accommodating. As well as fees, it receives vital donations from benefactors, and one in particular: Gerald French. The well-known businessman and public figure is a very generous supporter, who doesn't like to speak about - and even covers up - his involvement in keeping this establishment going. It might as well be called Gerald French House, so central has that man been to the lives of its young residents. In fact, his own son, Aaron, spent a few months at the establishment some years back.

On the face of it, the place is a godsend to parents who have tried everything they can to rekindle the passion for life that has abandoned their beloved sons and daughters. Maybe these children are desperately unhappy and don't know why, or maybe they refuse to eat and are wasting away. They might be angry with the world and unable to control their feelings or perhaps they are scared of it and want to hide away permanently. Or they might have another complaint, one that, every now and again, a parent, usually a father, even in these civilised times, will not tolerate. It is still the 1990s and although there are few stigmas left, and society is perfectly accepting, some young people have a fight on their hands when they want to tell the truth about their sexuality. These few cannot expect to be understood by their parents and there is no immediate community where they can seek friendship and inclusion. They are led to believe that they can be cured, straightened up, put back on the right course, and that there are individuals who are so skilled as to be able to recalibrate their minds. Most of the rest of society would be shocked to learn that this takes place within the neat brick walls of this Victorian house some way down a country lane in Berkshire. But then society doesn't know about it. Half of the residents in Yew Lodge don't even know about it.

Only those who need to know about it, know about it.

The therapy is so effective – harshly effective, but that's the way of these things – that it can inspire a man to be generous and reach out to help others with his money. He can contribute to the recalibration of the minds of other sons and daughters too. Not publicly. No need for a song and dance. Keep the names out of the press. But *your* money could eventually straighten out hundreds of confused young people and put them back on the right track. And wouldn't that have been a great thing to have done? That's greatness. That's making your mark.

දෙන

Oh thank God. At last, a story.

7

DEIRDRA CALLED TO congratulate me on my front
page byline.

"How awful" she exclaimed. "I had no idea such things
happened in this day and age. Those poor young people. That
bastard."

I had been working on the story for about a month and
in that time lawyers had come and gone anticipating the
legal kick-back and the furore from the French family. Gerald
French denied everything. Yew Lodge denied everything. But
I managed to dig up twelve individuals who either knew of
the controversial therapy or had been the victim of it – two
so traumatised by the process of conversion, that they could
barely bring themselves to describe it. I had even gone there
and confronted the ex-monk – Michael Sonder – and seen
the pink walls and beanbags for myself, heard the muted
chatter of the young residents who had been whisked away on
my arrival.

I hadn't told anybody about it because Guy told me not
to. Jay knew, of course, because he was a close colleague and
senior enough to be let in on the story.

Simon found out the day the story ran.

"How distasteful," he said. "I hate the thought of you
writing that filth."

He seemed to think this was some kind of gutter press
exposé and that I'd lowered myself to get it.

"But aren't you glad that I might have stopped something so cruel? And by someone so powerful?"

"They hand out halos in the pay packet, do they?"

I wasn't angry or hurt. I felt guilty. Yes, I really did. I felt like he had seen through me and taken note of my excessive pride. Why did I do this? To be of use to the public? Or to gratify a deeper need to be admired and considered of value? Had *that* been driving me all along?

Fortunately, Deirdra didn't ask what it meant to my ambitions, but took the story at face value (as I hoped any normal person would). Jay had a different approach still. He was interested in my rising stock in the office and was pleased for me.

At the pub a few days afterwards, we discussed follow-ups and responsibilities.

"I hope he's proud of you," he said, to bring the subject to a close.

I knew he meant Simon, though I didn't want to hear his name in this setting.

"He thinks I'm getting above myself."

He looked like he might have an opinion on that but took a mouthful of beer instead and kept his thoughts to himself.

"So, what are the plans?" he asked. "Going to work your way around Fleet Street? Get a nice columnist job somewhere and build your profile, that kind of thing? The BBC?"

And then, quietly, he added:

"Why are you here?"

It was October and the pub was packed and warm and damp. It was the modest crowning moment of my spectacular few days at the office. To be with him, hidden. To be close to him, anonymous. As usual, we'd waited for our corner to come free, had stood at the bar with our eyes trained on it. Once we were settled, the rest of the world disappeared.

"I've always loved this paper," I told him. "My aunt read it. I grew up on it. To work for it has been part of a cherished life-plan, if you like."

"Cherished life-plan," he muttered.

"What?"

"It's just a paper."

"Yes, but it's more than that. To work my way up, to make a name for myself, to build contacts, that will help me enter politics. It will give me everything I need. And then . . . and then everything can really start. Oh, you don't want to hear all this again."

He shrugged. "I'm happy to hear it again."

And there it was, the softness of the man, the humanity. Why hadn't I seen it at first? Why had he originally irritated me? Maybe it was nothing to do with him at all. Maybe I'd just felt an obligation to resist him. He had a blue V-necked jumper on over his striped shirt – clearly his autumn to winter outfit – and I don't know why, but the sight of him in it produced in me a kind of melting gratitude. An appetite and an aspiration to belong to him. There was a rightness to it. A *himness*.

"You're a bit married to this paper as well, though, aren't you?" I tried.

"Suppose I am."

"You're very good at what you do."

"Maybe. Yes, I probably am. I don't know."

"You are."

"I didn't mean all that," he said, glumly regarding his two-third-empty pint glass. I smiled at the sight of him. He was like a dog looking stupidly, yet endearingly, into a bowl. "I meant, what are you doing here, in this pub, with me?"

I opened my mouth, wanted to say so much, but didn't dare. I had a boyfriend at home who was even then waiting for me to come back so that he could function again. So, I tried to move all attention away from me.

"What do *you* want anyway? In life, I mean."

"Me?" He supressed a burp, kept his eyes on the wedge of gold at the bottom of his glass.

"Yes, you," I smiled.

"Me?"

I was laughing.

"Yes, *you*, you idiot."

He raised his eyes to mine.

"I want to shag you. I've wanted to shag you from the moment I saw you. I want to shag you so much tonight."

I looked at him. He looked at me. I began to cry.

"What?" he cried, panicked. "What is it?"

He parked his pint glass hurriedly, moved around the table and knelt in front of me, desolate, agonised.

Through the tears I told him: "I don't want to have an affair."

"No, God, no. Of course you don't. I'm sorry. I'm so sorry.

"But I so want to shag you, too."

And he put his hands – his huge, ugly, perfectly masculine hands – on my thighs, and looked directly in my face, and we both broke into the saddest laughter.

We spent the rest of the evening dejected and yet elated. How can that be?

We sat in silence, me leaning against him and I knew that – idiot of idiots! – I had made a fundamental mistake when it came to my love life. This was where I wanted to be, close up against the blue V-necked jumper. Was it too late to change course?

Back home, waiting for me, cooking our dinner, concentrating as he does it, with the radio on and one hand, as ever, stuffed in the back pocket of his loose jeans, is a man whose every day is dependent on me being there. I have given him a home and provided the missing piece for his life plan. When I step through that door, everything becomes possible for him again. But what if I don't? How will he cope? Will it be the last straw in a life already battered by the thoughtlessness of others?

But what about *him*, close against me, silly-drunk, unable to work out why everything suddenly hurts so much. Wanting me. Wanting to fuck me. What about him?

No, you are not beautiful, Jay Corey, with your bull neck and your stumpy hands. Your coarse hair and your bleached rugby shirts. There's nothing remotely pre-Raphaelite about you. You are not different or exceptional. No one would look twice at you in the street. You are like a thousand other men. You shout and you probably fight. There is nothing subtle or hidden about you. You want to do your job well and you fancy me now because I have done mine well.

There is nothing at all enigmatic about you. You say what you feel, you expose your heart, like a fool. Like a total fucking idiot.

I want you so much.

I want you so, so much. You are mine. Beloved. To be adored, to be clung to. No one is like you. No one comes close to how magnificent you are. I want to put my arms around you and lay my head on that mattress of a chest of yours and I never want to let you go.

Agony and euphoria. How can that be?

Was it simply that I had never really been in love before?

※

I continued crying all the way home and was crying, still, as I went up the steps to the top of my building and let myself in, and I cried as I sat down on my sofa and pointed the remote at the telly.

"Where have you been?" I heard Simon's voice behind me. I could smell that he was just out of the bath and was in his dressing gown.

I wouldn't turn around.

"Si," I said. "I'm sorry."

"What about?"

For once in your life, step up.

"About the fact that we're just not right for each other."

He was breathing heavily through his nose. I could hear it. "What?"

I had said all I needed to say. I couldn't actually believe I had said it but it was out and I had to face the consequences.

He sat down beside me on the sofa. Took the remote out of my hands and switched the telly off.

"Now, what's brought this on, eh? Are you a bit mad at me because I wasn't in awe of that big scoop of yours? You know I'm proud. I'm sorry I didn't say it. I just had an unproductive day. Some days I produce bloody gold dust. Other days ain't so good. That's what you get when you shack up with a writer."

I didn't know where I should clip this conversation to cut it off and end it. I wasn't going to achieve anything.

He reached out for me and I knew I was expected to climb onto his lap.

I'm sure I loved you once. I must have. Did I? Why are we here together if I didn't?

I couldn't move and wouldn't go closer to him.

"Listen," he said. "I've been thinking a lot. I know what it is. I know what's bugging you. I'm not a total moron."

I looked at him in utter bewilderment. How could he know? Did he see it in me? Did what I felt for Jay show itself on my face or produce some kind of giveaway odour?

"If you really want to get married, then let's do it," he said. "I had it all planned and I was going to ask you properly at the book launch. In front of everyone. Girls like that, right?"

What book launch?

"Si," I said. "Didn't you hear me?"

He paused, controlled himself, then shook his head. He couldn't talk to me just then, needed me to catch up with him. He left me in the living room to think about things.

☙

In bed, I moved as far away from him as possible. I couldn't bear for him to touch me. I thought it had worked and that he was going to go to sleep but he shuffled close to me and I felt his breath on the back of my neck.

"Do you remember how we walked home that night," he said in a low, urgent monotone. "Do you remember how we felt?"

I muttered that I did.

"I knew then that I had found my soul mate. And I know you felt it, too. Couples have their ups and downs, but we're different. We're meant to be together."

I would have said something then, if I'd had known what. He reached round and found my hand and held it.

"I've been pushed around and damaged all my life," he told me. "I have absolutely no family but you. You've given me strength and love and support. No one else understands me like you do. You're my muse, chicky. You're what keeps me going."

I didn't know what to say. I squeezed his hand. I shouldn't have. It signalled that I understood and that he was right and it gave him the courage to tell me as an end to this silliness: "Anyway, this is my home now. My everything. And I'm not leaving it."

8

I WAS NOW crying a lot of the time. Not in public, but as soon as I could escape everyone's attention.

I cried because I couldn't carry the burden of hurting Simon. For the rest of that week we lived together in silence, him sulking with his books, me pressed against the edge of the flat as though I wanted to sink into its walls and find myself somewhere between them and the outside world. I agreed with Jay that I wouldn't go to the pub with him for a while – if ever again. To be near him at work was as painful as to be at home.

And maybe there was an upside to the crying, professionally-speaking, because I was so engaged in it, albeit covertly, that I didn't notice that I was being given interesting work and that I was carrying it out more than adequately. Since the Yew Lodge scandal, I found that the stories were coming to me and not needing to be looked for.

Deirdra called me at work.

"Well done you," she said. "Saw the latest byline. You're on a roll."

"Oh yeah, forgot about that. It's not a big deal."

If she wanted a return on her enthusiasm, she was destined to be disappointed.

"You a tad low, darlin'?

"Just a tad."

I told her a little about the conversation with Simon.

About how he'd been planning to ask me to marry him and about how much he needed me.

"And he won't leave?"

"No. He says it's the first place that's ever felt like home to him. I can't ask him to go. Anyway, we haven't really split up as such."

"What kind of relationship can you have now, though? Now that you've told him you're not right for each other?"

I didn't realise until that point that I could feel any lower.

"I can't talk about this now. Sorry."

"I shall seek advice," she said.

"No, no, please don't interfere, Deirdra, please."

My poor, eternally enthused aunt. There's always an answer. Someone will have a solution, someone holds the key. But this was my fault and I had to sort it out. If I had the heart for it. Who on earth was Deirdra going to get to fix it? What immutably practical world did she live in and why couldn't I inhabit one like that, too?

Somehow, I had to find the courage to ask myself some questions and force myself to act on the answers. It was no one's business but mine.

I didn't confide in Jay though we were now yearning so powerfully for each other that it felt like a physical illness. I'm sure that our colleagues noticed what was going on. How can you hide such a thing? All I said was that Simon refused to move out and he merely listened to the fact and tried not to weigh in. He thought he was being fair and generous and solicitous. I just wanted him to take me away.

I worked late at the end of that week. I was part of a team investigating claims about historic sexual abuse at a children's home in the Midlands. I seemed to have made a name for myself by exposing the cruel treatment of young people. It's funny how these things happen. I never went looking for it. As awful as these stories were, they gave me a reputation for honourableness and dignity. The paper liked the idea that it didn't just expose wrong-doing: it had a heart, too. A crusading, selfless, *female* heart. *We can get attached to these issues*, said the paper. *We are not above emotion. And we have a nice young woman reporter who proves it.*

I was getting call after call from people who wanted to talk. Each call was a long-held-in moment of honesty and unburdening that might never have happened were it not for our research. With each one I had to listen to a litany of unpleasantness and let the talker get to the end of the story. I had to reach out and try to understand without taking the burden onto my own shoulders. *I am a conduit*, I would tell them rather pompously. *I will tell your story to the best of my abilities.*

But my abilities were hampered by the fact that I was breaking apart. Each awful detail weighed on my crammed heart. Each story of brutality struck home because of my own guilt. When I listened to these men – and they usually were men – Simon's was the image before my eyes.

Every time that phone rang, I took it personally.

On the Friday night, after a week of this, I felt unable to move.

Jay came and found me at my desk, the other reporters long gone, the news desk handover and the pub trip accomplished some time ago. Without a word, we left the office together and walked towards the Tube.

It was nearly the end of the year and intensely cold – minus figures. I remember how wrapped up I was against the icy wind. Jay was in an overcoat, but it wasn't even buttoned up and I focused on his frayed shirt collar. I reached out and rubbed the edge of it with my thumb and laughed through my tears. He caught my wrist and said: "I can't bear this."

I couldn't either.

"I can't take the pain of it," he told me. "I don't do well in this kind of situation."

He was talking about his ex-wife, I guessed. I didn't know the details, but I understood that he'd been deeply wounded and that he'd told himself he wouldn't go there again. But what could I do? And anyway – what did he want from me? Wasn't I suffering enough as well?

"One minute I'm fine and getting on with my life and and then I'm told 'look at the new girl. Isn't she cute! Why don't you mentor her?' And now look!"

"Cute?" I exclaimed. "Don't be ridiculous. No one said that."

"Yes, he did. Cute. And you are."

"I'm being torn apart," I told him. (That's the kind of language we used then.) "I feel so utterly miserable about all this."

He pulled me into a side road and we kissed and I cried and it occurred to me that maybe we could stay there for ever. But he was tense and needed an end to all this.

"What I'm saying is that if you can't leave him, then we can't continue like this."

He was demanding an answer or a release. But I stumbled over my words, didn't know what was allowed to be said out loud, what would devastate us.

"He's been hurt so much for so long," I told him glumly. "I can't. I can't do this to him. Not at the moment. I need to be kind to him. And anyway, he doesn't seem to get it."

"It's not being kind," Jay murmured.

And then of course my phone rang.

"Fuck," he said.

"I have to take it. I'm sorry."

He kissed me and turned away.

I don't think I've ever been so grateful for a kiss or so confused by one.

I took the call.

"Hello?"

"I've seen your name in the paper. We know what you want. Please leave us alone."

I didn't know what to make of it. Looked to Jay for an explanation, as though he could answer every single query in my life.

"I'm sorry?" I said. "Who is this please?"

"Kim Gartner. You left me a message."

Jay was moving off. I was shaking my head, reaching out, trying to stop him.

"Wait! Please!"

She thought I was talking to her.

"This is just to ask you – please – to not call us again. My father isn't very well. And besides we've done absolutely nothing wrong."

He was beyond my reach now. I saw his broad back fold itself among the other bodies at the Tube entrance. Cars rushed by, the wind seemed able to cut through me even under my many layers. Deep, deep deposits of self-pity were crowding up and reaching my throat.

I was alone and didn't understand a single thing.

"I'm sorry," I said to her, faintly.

And now neither one of us understood the other.

"So?" she asked.

"So?"

"Will you kindly leave us alone. We can't help you."

I watched body after body get swallowed up by the Underground. Thick coats bumped against each other like balls in an arcade game.

He was gone.

"I was her friend," I said to nobody in particular. "I kept watch one night with her. That's all. That's all I have to say. This is nothing to do with a story. I wanted to know if she's still – "

The older sister, the one who sent the hampers and packages to her younger sibling to get her through her difficult university days, who kept us in Baileys that night, was – I knew – calculating how much to tell me. Protective to the last.

"Still alive?" she asked.

Stupidly, I nodded. She ended the emptiness by putting the phone down.

❧

I had a recurring dream, in those days, and it was so vivid that it happened as much when I was awake and drifting as when I was unconscious.

I was asleep – in this dream – and aware of it. And then I opened my eyes and saw mist or steam – hot, damp uncomfortable air that hung in the room around me. I pushed myself up from a bed on which I had been lying and the mist dispersed to reveal an open window. I couldn't bear to see the wide expanse of dangerous sky, nothing between it and me. I moved forward until I reached it and I grabbed the windowsill and forced myself to look over the edge.

She was always there. Lying in a variety of poses, maybe her arms out to the sides or her legs folded beneath her, but always face up and although I was looking at her from many floors above, I could see her expression.

And it was always smiling.

※

Jay's receding back was the insistent image before my eyes as I headed home that night. The rest - the news story, the call from Danielle's sister - none of it seemed able to hold my attention. I cradled the impossibility of my situation all the way home on the Tube and then in the train, pushed up against people who were clearly tired and yet seemed so much lighter than me. I've always felt that Friday night commuters move like a battalion at the end of a long campaign, smelling freedom, trudging home with the last ounce of energy, aware of all the new possibilities. I looked around me on the train and, for the first time, felt I wasn't one of the pack any more. They were moving in one direction and I was being swept away in the other.

When I came out of the station, the evening air seemed so sharp and remedial. I could maybe spend the whole night walking, pacing through streets I didn't know, looking through windows at other people's lives. That wouldn't be weird, would it?

But my feet led me home, even if my will was pushing me to go in the opposite direction. Until that moment in my life, I had never had a heavier heart. If I sound flippant about it now, almost nostalgic, then I do my past self a disservice. I was aching almost beyond endurance. I remember that, as I walked up the hill, I pictured myself stepping in front of one of the passing cars, and I braced myself. Shocked myself. How had I reached such a point? It was all my own doing and now I didn't have the wherewithal to undo any of it.

At the top of the hill, the house stood dark against the evening sky. The ground floor lights were off. From down there my top floor windows weren't visible. I opened the main door and stood in the hallway, looking up the carpeted stairs. He was always home, didn't have any kind of social life without me. He would be waiting now, probably in the bath with a book propped up on the rack and an empty mug on the floor beside him. Our dinner would be in the oven, the table set.

On my way up, I passed Abi and Kate's flat on the first floor. I could hear music, heard Kate calling out to Abi to hurry up or the taxi would be there. They were going out. Of course they were, it was Friday night. For a second I thought I might knock and ask to join them. Or maybe I could just sit there in their flat while they were out. I wanted them to see my sore eyes, to wonder at the forlorn state of me and cancel their plans and tend to me instead. I wanted to park myself between them on their sofa, like I used to in those easiest of times, and to listen to their chatter and slowly return to the admirably inane, peacefully positive person I had recently left off being.

Who would look after me and turn me around and point me in the right direction? I ached for my mother, then, or for a sister who would place her hand on me and absorb all my anguish and nullify it. Who was watching over me? No one. Who was out there this busy, heartless night who might care for me and tell me what to do?

I carried on, took those further two flights of stairs haltingly, and arrived at the door to my flat, my fingers falling lightly on the keys in my pocket, not quite able to grasp them.

How sick he will be of the sight of my red eyes, I told myself. I waited for them to dry and wiped my nose on my sleeve. *Breathe in, breathe out, be nice. Be nice.*

I opened the front door and stood and listened for the sound of fingers tapping at a keyboard. He was nearly always at the screen when I got back, usually preoccupied and undemonstrative. He needed to unwind, he always said, before leaving his words behind and giving me attention.

I didn't hear anything and there was something different about the place. It *felt* different. The air was different. The smell was different. It smelt clean. It smelt empty.

Things had gone. But what things? In the living room, the sofa was still there and the table against the wall and the telly, but his guitars were no longer around, or that awful carved wooden statue. The rug he'd brought with him from his childhood bedroom was also missing. There was nothing cooking in the kitchen, nothing set on the table.

I moved on into the bedroom, my pace picking up as I grasped what was going on. I stood in the doorway and scanned the room. The wall beside the bed was empty. The books had gone. My sewing table was bare and pushed back where it had once been. Jesus Christ – all his things had gone! I rushed to the bathroom.

He wasn't there.

I put down the toilet lid, sat and listened.

The place felt cavernous. This tiny aperture of a home, this pocket of a space that I'd occupied for three years was now positively an arena again. Simon had left it. He'd taken

126

everything that was his and moved himself on. And he'd done it in a rush and clumsily, I guessed, because there was a slight smear of his blood on the edge of the bath.

I got up, reached for the bath sponge, and wiped it away.

PART THREE

1

CAITLIN HAD TRANSFORMED the room.

In all the time it belonged to her predecessor, Geoff Mattison, it had been utilitarian in appearance, with a desk, a couple of chairs, some reference books on a single shelf and a yellowish-greyish, inescapable tobacco pall. As soon as Caitlin English was appointed editor, she had the place fumigated, re-painted and hung with over-large art works. There was a cryptic pink plastic article on her desk that was rumoured to be by a Young British Artist and to be worth thousands but was an object of ridicule in the newsroom.

I'd visited Geoff on several occasions in that unremarkable and unpleasant-smelling chamber and had a few vigorous and enjoyable conversations with him, while he coughed and spluttered with a gritty laughter that must have hurt coming out. I feared him in my early months at *The Messenger*, but we grew playful with each other and eventually I found myself telling new recruits what I, too, had been told (and not believed at the time): that he was a pussycat. Illness and age forced him out, but he went with a solid reputation and nothing much that could be held against him.

Caitlin came of different stock. She'd edited the women's section of a rival paper and had written a semi-academic book on the death of print media and was considered entirely the right fit for the paper: the intelligent, well-educated career woman who could broaden its outlook. And, what's more, someone mildly influential who could be interviewed by the BBC without making a fool of herself or her employers. She wore white suits, which I'd never come across in a workplace before, and, fair's fair, she wore them well. Her hair was white-blond and short, her brows very dark. Her waist was narrower than my youngest child's.

On the day she called me to her room, I had been idly tidying my desk in readiness. I knew I was going soon and, although I didn't want to draw attention to myself, it excited me to be putting a few things in my handbag – just making a symbolic start. I got a message on my phone to come and see her at once.

The newsroom was lively that morning. There were fewer staff these days and more young ones. The new balance of personalities and generations brought with it a kind of serenity. Younger people supplied the blunt energy necessary to unearth stories but also the humour and hubris to question what they were told. I loved their company and had mentored quite a number of trainees over the years. I walked among the desks without greeting anyone or catching any eyes and arrived at the double doors, through which Guy Thornsbeech propelled me that first morning after my job interview. How enormous the newsroom had seemed to me then.

The corridor was empty except for a cleaner who was wiping down the walls. Her bucket and mop stood a little further down from her. I greeted her with a flat smile, which she returned, and I knocked on the editor's door.

"Yes! Do come in!"

I entered a place of startling colour, like a small gallery, with white walls bearing large canvases of boldly slashed paint. A yellow Perspex coffee table was strewn with magazines and journals. Her large desk was host not only to documents, letters and books but also framed photographs, perfume bottles, scarves and handbags.

I wondered: is this your home? Am I allowed to defile it by coming in?

She was in a sleeveless beige blouse and white trousers. The room was very hot, presumably to make these clothes wearable on a November morning. She'd been standing on her white rug but now moved back to sit behind her desk. She indicated a large turquoise sofa on which I sat down and I smiled briskly and enquiringly at her. She could speak first.

Of course, that's what she intended. She barely hesitated.

"I've literally just come out of a board meeting where I got a humiliating bollocking. They tore me to shreds."

"Oh no." Beside me, on the sofa, was a cushion which I picked up and held against me.

"Do you know why?" she said.

"Why?"

She took a deep breath, her eyes never leaving my face. Her brows were extraordinary, I thought. Were they drawn on?

"Because of your letter."

I held the cushion a little tighter.

"Oh."

"Yes, 'Oh'. They say it's my fault that you want to go and that I'm not to allow it."

I was older than Caitlin by about five years. I wasn't prepared to be made to feel younger. The tiredness that had characterised the last few years at *The Messenger* for me was yet again making itself felt. I'm sure it showed on my face.

"I'm not allowed to go?"

"You know what I mean. Of course you're allowed to go

but they don't *want* you to. I was told very clearly that you're doing such a sterling job as political editor that it would damage our reputation to lose you."

"I'm not, though."

"You're not what?"

"I'm not doing a sterling job. You and I both know that. I'm doing an OK job. There are at least three very talented and hard-working journalists out there who could pick up from me without a second thought."

"Oh, come on."

I wasn't sure if she was exasperated with me or the board or the world, or what. She tapped a hard caramel-brown fingernail against her desktop.

"How long have you been here?" she asked, by way of a new avenue of appeal.

"At *The Messenger*? Twenty-four years. As political editor, eight."

"Eight is nothing."

"Eight is plenty. Before that I was the political writer and before that a home affairs reporter. And before that a kind of crimes-against-society writer, or whatever. I've done it now. Let someone else do it."

Even this room exhausted me. Twenty-four years of seeming confident but always looking over my shoulder, wondering what would come next. I didn't go into an editor's room, even at my senior level, without losing something of my minimal advantage. Like a schoolgirl. Like a student standing before her impatient tutor.

"Hmm." Caitlin's expression was darkening, her brows and forehead crowding. "In that time you've done some good work. Toppled a public figure or two. Some staggeringly good stories have fallen into your lap."

I almost laughed. She was goading me. Trying to diminish my few achievements on the paper.

"Stories always fall into reporters' laps. That's how it works. Otherwise we'd be making them up."

"You know what I mean."

"No, I don't."

"You've had some lucky breaks."

"Yes, I have, haven't I?"

I didn't have the patience for this. I didn't fear her or fear for my career. I could go right now, if I wanted to. They didn't own me. I had worked hard to get my senior positions, and been patient, too, which is just as important. It's not how the stories come to you, it's what you do with them. Anyway, what did she know about hard news? Nothing.

"What does Jay think?" she asked.

I tilted my head by way of telling her that it was none of her business.

She must have thought I didn't understand her.

"I mean, about your packing it in so young? Doesn't he think it a travesty? Besides, isn't it nice still working together? I'd love to see Hugh at work every day."

"I'm 48."

"And that's your answer?"

"I'm not young, Caitlin. As for Jay, he supports me in everything. Anyway, he's chief sub now. That's a brilliant achievement – he worked part-time for years, looking after the kids while they were little. It's his turn to progress his career. And my turn to spend a bit of time at home."

And then to place a full stop on any explanation I was expected to give, I told her:

"This is not a decision I've come to easily. As a girl I set my sights on working on this paper. It was my dream job."

"And dreams evaporate?"

"No," I told her. "But old dreams make way for other dreams. I need to move on."

There was a further distortion of the brows as though she were watching me disintegrate before her eyes and couldn't find the words.

She bit her lip while contemplating her next move.

"May I confide something in you?" she asked at last.

I signalled that it was fine by me.

"I feel like an imposter," she said. "All the time. I've been here two solid years and yet it feels like I'm standing in for someone. I was on *Newsnight* last night. Did you see me? Outside this paper I'm a somebody, a recognisable figure in the industry. And yet I tremble every day at the thought of how I might run this paper into the ground, with everyone laughing around me and saying: *I told you so. She was the wrong choice. Weak. She's too weak.*

"When it comes to this job – this vaunted, hallowed bloody job – I don't think I deserve it and I don't believe I've earned it."

I pushed myself to the edge of the sofa, still hugging the cushion, still feeling instinctively that I needed to shield myself.

"Why are you telling me this?"

I was in her sights now.

"Because you know exactly what I mean."

There it hung, between us.

Was this a late attempt as feigning friendship? Or was it an indulgent farewell attack? *If I have to suffer with a job that's beyond me, why should I let you escape yours?*

I was in no rush to respond. The woman didn't like me. Possibly didn't like a whole lot of women who worked there. Caitlin was on the backfoot all the time but instead of seeking and making friendships, she wanted others – people she deduced were as shaky as her – to struggle along beside her and feel the daily disquiet that she felt. It was how she operated, but I wouldn't rise to anything and I wouldn't act as if she'd understood me or seen some greater truth about us. And so I put the cushion aside, and got up, not wounded, no, not even minded to counter anything or to show any emotion at all. I just wanted to leave and she had given me a good enough reason to do so. I cleared my throat and toyed with telling her that I was bored and tired with the whole Westminster beat, that I was writing the same stories in a loop year after year, that when it came to choosing between my job and being at home with my family, it was the easiest decision of my life. I shouldn't have said anything, but I did. I said to her:

"I thought you said you wanted me to stay here."

She finally dropped her gaze from me and found something of interest on her desk. She picked up a sheet of paper and examined it. Caitlin produced a smile before she dismissed me:

"I didn't," she said. "I told you that *they* wanted you to stay. Not me."

⁂

I saw him across the room and I lingered because I wasn't sure how much more often I would be able to enjoy the sight. Jay Corey, chief sub of *The Messenger*, scourge of the lazy journalist, the clueless writer, the hopeless speller. Solid, full of life and noise and brimming with latent mischief and bonhomie. My husband. Father of my three children. Let me say soulmate, however hackneyed an idea it might be. Mate, anyway. For the last 24 years, on and off depending on our employment contract at the time, I had crossed the newsroom like this and gone to see him. At first it was a thing of delicious indiscretion, two colleagues who were sleeping together, continuing the secret flirtation. And then officially a couple, rather indulged by our workmates who were charmed by the romance playing out in front of them. Then ignored, our marriage a piece of the paper's folklore, almost a lucky talisman and a reassuring presence. And all the great milestones of our life together – our marriage, the purchase of our house, the birth of our three children – all passed by as daytime gossip in our workplace, knowing its place beside our professional progress and daily duties.

His sleeves were pushed up, of course, his shirt half hanging out. His tie not quite centred. His bare arms still filled me with longing, even then, because they signalled the strength of him. They held me and they held my babies and they seemed only to grow more reassuring over the years. My God, I couldn't get past him in the kitchen without a furtive squeeze of a tit, or a slap on the arse. Couldn't go up the stairs without him feeling compelled to chase me. And my own hands still always had to find him in the night; to feel the life of him, to know he was there, to realise that he wanted me as much as I wanted him. It was a *phenomenon*, the reality of us, the complex yet easy arrangement that was our love and our physical life together.

I watched him for a moment, took in the familiar stance, the usual expression. He was standing over a colleague and they were scratching their heads and finding something amusing on a screen.

What drives you? How do you maintain that essence of strength and competence that runs through you? I'll never see a sight more precious than you, here, now. No one – not even our youngest child – belongs so wholly to me as you do.

As soon as he saw me, he left the others with a "hang on a sec" and met me halfway.

"How did it go?"

"Strange."

That frown, that amused pout. It was like looking in a mirror. More familiar to me, perhaps, than looking at my own face.

"Good strange or bad strange?"

I wished I could at least touch him. But never at work, that was the law.

"Neither. She didn't believe me that I wanted to pack it all in."

He shrugged.

"No one finds her easy to deal with. You're not the only one."

I fell onto the nearest chair.

"Is it me, or does it feel funny here today?"

He parked himself on the edge of a desk, folded his arms, pulled a face.

"No funnier than usual."

"It must be me, then. It must be the thought of leaving, of moving on. It's scary. A bit. Like losing someone who looked over me."

"Yeah," he said, also lost in the pregnancy of the moment. "That's how these places work, I suppose. But . . ."

I raised my face to him, waiting for his help, wasn't expecting a question.

"Are you really sure?" he asked.

Was I sure? Hadn't I convinced him successfully enough over the past year that my last dregs of ambition at that paper had evaporated? Hadn't he listened as I outlined all the times when I came close to cocking up and having to leave? Couldn't he see how tired I was, how wide of the mark all this was? More than twenty years of doubt and anxiety, of expecting any moment to be found out and sent on my way. I carried with me a permanent sense that I owed my success to dogged persistence, making the right friends, generally being likeable, and simply hanging around. Not because I was brilliant at my job. And now I wanted to go home. I wanted to be good at something at last.

"I'm sure," I told him.

He nodded and I saw in his eyes that apologetic devotion that still humbled me and which was the only thing that ever filled me with any confidence in the face of a puzzling world.

"Then bugger off," he said. "I've got a paper to get out."

I couldn't touch him, I couldn't kiss him. I smiled. He winked. That would have to do.

On the way back to my desk I got a call from my daughter's school. She'd been sent home – again. I texted Jay to tell him and, with a new-found disregard for working hours, grabbed my handbag and headed back to the house.

2

OWNSTAIRS, THE RADIATORS were on and the house felt warm and occupied. It was a relief to know Willa was there and not wandering in a park somewhere or taking one of her bus journeys around London. I listened for her as I took off my coat and dropped my bag. Nothing downstairs. She had to be in her room.

She was on her bed, the dog in the crook of her arm, her hair over her face, her music in her ears. I indicated for her to remove the ear buds.

Standing above her, I looked down at my youngest child, those dark eyes exactly like her father's, that round, clear, permanently mystified face far more like my own.

"You OK?"

She nodded. I sat down on the edge of the bed.

"What?" she asked with the usual defensive aggression of her age. The dog eyed me as though I were a danger to both of them.

"Why are you home?"

She freed her arm from the dog and rolled over to face the wall and so I held back.

Eventually, she spoke, talking to the duvet, rather than directly to me.

"There was no point to today."

"Does there have to be a point to every day?"

"Of course there has to be a point. Don't try and talk like you understand."

I felt the usual time-stopping that occurs with a teenage assault. Do I discuss this? Do I just stroke that sleek and tousled head and let it be? God, someone! Tell me what to do!

But she turned back to me and quelled something inside her.

"I'm not sure I could have got through the day there, not without crying or something. And that would be embarrassing, and people would ask what was the matter with me and I wouldn't want to say. So I came home."

"OK." And I did stroke the head after all.

This wasn't the first time she had upped and left school, citing the pointlessness of it. Willa, our baby, was unlike her brother and sister in every way, but most particularly in her casual contempt for rules and conventions. It was almost as though she saw through them and they bored her. Everything and everyone had the propensity to let her down and she felt the teachery of that letting-down. Tess and Theo might have been livelier and more demanding as babies and toddlers, but Willa, the quiet and subdued young child, had grown into the more complicated human being on reaching adolescence. Her siblings went off to university and now she was alone and with too much time to examine her heart and her place in the world. My role, it seemed clear to me, was to distract her from herself in the hope that she would achieve, in time, a calmer maturity. But both Jay and I knew that Willa was unlikely to grow out of her peculiarly negative world view any time soon and it scared us. There was something excruciating inside her and I couldn't find a way of easing it.

But she was gentle and almost invisible at home. And she dearly loved me.

Moments of aggression were followed by reparations.

"So, did you resign?" she asked.

"I did. And brought the world down on my head."

Her interest was piqued and she sat up. The dog jumped off the bed and left.

"What will you do now?"

"Good question. I'll work my notice, of course, and after that, well, I thought I might just stop. I know stopping was not part of the plan but . . . but I don't want to do anything right now. Just stop."

"Oh yeah. The great plan."

She shuffled forwards and ended up with her arms around me, her head flat against my chest.

How I love you, my beautiful girl. How I wish I could get to the bottom of your disquiet.

I talked to the top of her head, spilling all my thoughts, hoping they didn't irritate her. Anything could set her off.

"Do you remember me telling you about that weird bloke I used to live with, before I met Dad?"

A muffled "yeah".

"I've been thinking about him, and how he planned things all the time. But I think he was too scared to actually do any of it. He talked the talk, I'm afraid. Funny, but I bought into it. I think that when he said we were the best of our generation I really wanted to believe it. What he actually wanted was to be looked after and protected and he wanted to marry me just to keep me on board."

"Narrow escape."

"I know."

"What happened to him?" she asked.

"That's a good question. He just walked out on me when I made it clear that we weren't meant to be. Packed up his stuff while I was out and disappeared. I tracked down his mother and she just apologised and said that was him all over. Self-obsessed."

"Where did he go?"

"I've always assumed abroad. She called me a couple of times to see if he'd been in touch with me, but he hadn't. Weird isn't it, when someone disappears and no one actually cares."

"Imagine not being cared about."

"Indeed."

I felt the arms tighten around my ribcage.

"But I don't want to leave you. I don't want to go to university."

"Then don't. It's your choice."

And we sat like that for a while. I had learnt to let any small flurry of anxiety slowly drain away. I couldn't talk anxiety out of her; we had to be patient and to do it together. Minutes passed and she righted herself. I was feeling constricted by her arms but didn't dare hurt her feelings by pulling free. When her words came, they came from very close to my chest. It could have been me speaking.

"Mum, I know what you think of me."

"Do you?" I said. "Go on, then. Let's see if you're anywhere near."

She was tense. I could feel it in her arms.

"You think – *why did I even bother?*"

I stroked her back.

"No, I don't."

"You think, there I was with a daughter and then a son and they got on with each other fine and then I went and had another one and the pattern was ruined and she's been really annoying ever since and now I'm saddled with her."

Really annoying.

I think of the little criss-crosses on her inner arms, faded now but remaining as a testament to how *really annoying* she could be. Annoying! Jay and I cried the night we discovered them, heads together in bed, wondering aloud whether this hasty action or that moment of discipline led to her despair. Because of course we assumed that there was some fault in our parenting that caused her to think so negatively. It had to be our fault.

Jay had instantly cut back his hours so that he could be with her as much as possible.

I remember the marvel of a SENCO at Willa's school who had seen it all before and who seemed more keen to comfort us than she did our daughter, maybe because she could foresee the trials still ahead. It was this level-headed individual who told me to accept things the way they were. "Some people have great trouble growing up," she said. "They don't want to and they will fight it all the way. Willa will get there eventually – it's just there's no knowing when."

"And in the meantime?" I'd said to her.

"In the meantime, listen to everything as though it were of earth-shattering importance and know that none of it is important."

"It's funny," she went on. "Once upon a time a child like that would have stayed in the family home and become a contented spinster, attached to her parents, not very interested in the world."

"A spinster! There's a big, beautiful world out there waiting for young people to discover! Why would I deny her that?"

"Maybe she's just not interested in the world. Maybe she's not you."

Willa's reclusive nature had made her a target in school and two unpleasant and vicious girls also made it their life's work to taunt her. The fact that she was academically gifted didn't make things easier. We did our best to separate her from her tormentors but they always seemed to find a way to reach her. In the end, we moved her to a different school but by then she believed the "weirdo" tag and assumed that she was meant to inhabit the fringes of life.

It was Jay who managed to get us beyond crisis. He was focused entirely on our children and noticed every storm far away on the horizon and prepared me for each one.

Now it was my turn to go storm-watching.

I wriggled out from my daughter's grasp and finally got to look at her petulant face.

"Listen, you. We're not going down that road today, OK? We had you because I desperately wanted another little idiot to add to my collection. And now you're a nice big idiot and my only idiot left at home, so we're going to enjoy being with each other."

She shrugged, tried to hide the strain in her heart.

"Like doing what?"

"Like all the little things we've loved doing together. Shopping, gardening, cooking, finishing sewing that jumpsuit you started eons ago. And studying for some A Levels and passing them."

"You'll get bored," she said simply. "And anyway, it's not part of your great life plan."

I got up, had an urge to tidy her room, started briskly on the mound of clothes on the floor, anything to stop her reaching out for me again. I loved to hold her, loved the feel of those arms around me, but she had to let go of me.

She pushed a little more.

"So is the plan all gone to fuck?"

"Nicely put. No, it's just being adjusted. A lovely person once told me that plans stay intact. They only need tweaking a bit."

She watched me tidying, used her foot to push an empty plate towards me in case I missed it.

"I don't see it," she said. "You're not a tweaker when it comes to life-plans."

༄

I never sold my flat on the hill.

Jay and I bought our house using the rent from my old place and by asking Jay's brother to buy him out of their flat they owned together. I'm not a hoarder, I can let go of things easily, but not that eyrie of a home, not that place where I was so happy in my solitude. I've often yearned for what it represented to me – those convivial years where I built up my reserves and prepared myself for a more important life. The knowledge that things wouldn't remain as simple and cheerful for ever made those few solo years all the more precious.

But, how strange is this: I can't bear the thought of living there again. I don't know why. The later associations, I suppose. There were plenty of perfectly happy days there with Simon but they have receded in my memory and the grim ones have remained. And his departure. That was a bump I couldn't flatten out. My initial joy at his disappearance – I rang Jay that very night and he came over and we discussed matters seriously and at just-about-bearable length before rushing into the bedroom – soon turned sour and wouldn't give me peace.

It had served me so well, this compact, restful, neutral place, when I first left my childhood home. It wouldn't work for what I wanted thereafter. Within two years of our marrying I was pregnant and I wanted a family home and to keep building on what we had. Not going back.

It would serve another young person well, so I rented it out and one day it could be used by my children, perhaps. In short, I couldn't let it go.

❧

Before I fully left *The Messenger*, I had to endure a leaving party.

By choice I would have run a mile from such a thing but, of course, that was impossible and Jay was going to be there so I had some moral support. It was paid for by *The Messenger* and held on the first floor of a wine bar in Victoria. Caitlin was organising it, which was why I didn't have the courage to oppose it. She told me to invite all my old contacts and she would do the rest. She wanted one more twist of torture for me before I could finally escape them all.

And so, on a windy night just before the Christmas of 2015, I found myself once more in my grey work trousers and black satin blouse, my mid-heels and pearl bracelet (formal get-up, in other words) standing among knots of Westminster and media folk with nothing but alcohol and a husband to keep me going.

Caitlin dragged me from group to group before taking shelter, each time, with her own husband and friends. This was her natural habitat, entertaining people and connecting them with each other as she did so. I had to admit there was a skill to it – one I wasn't blessed with.

"You'll know Selma, of course," she said pulling me to a woman in a canary-yellow wool dress and red stilettos.

"Of course," I said. "Hello, Selma. Thank you for coming."

"Thank you for giving me an excuse to leave the lobby tonight."

I should have known what was keeping her in the House late. Once I would have sparred with a politician or wheedled something out of her or simply used the opportunity to build on a relationship. Tonight, I didn't give a shit and I didn't have a clue.

Selma Henry was an exceptional MP. What's more she was my constituency MP, having served our corner of South East London for as long as I'd lived there. She was a little older than me, in her early-50s, very glamorous, charismatic, much-loved and looked up to. I had met her before, briefly, in the House, but never locally, strangely enough.

"So," said Selma, addressing me. "Are you writing an exposé or something? Or going into PR? What drags you away from the best paper in the land?"

Caitlin leapt in to answer on my behalf.

"Well, a little bird told me, Selma, that she's going into your line of work."

I was taken aback.

"No," I said at once. "Who told you that?"

"I'm sure you said it yourself. It's understood."

"Well, it's not understood," I told them. "I'm just going to

149

stop and take stock of my life. Slow down a bit."

Selma offered me a reassuring smile.

"I'm sure you'd make a wonderful MP," she said. "But you have to really want it. You can't just go into it half-cock."

"I agree," I told her. "And I wouldn't even be half-cock. I'd be quarter-cock. Actually, I'd be no cock at all!"

"Would you excuse me," said Caitlin, edging away. "Hugh is cornering that poor girl again."

Both Selma and I breathed a little more lightly once Caitlin had gone.

"Did you always know?" I asked her. "That you would stand for Parliament one day?"

"Oh, no," she said. Her lips were stained a deep reddish-purple, her eyelids a similar shade. Everything about her was admirably upbeat and secure. "Funnily enough my family were all journalists for generations. I started working in the NHS as a young woman and was active in the union and, well, it seemed to make sense to go into politics."

"You don't wish you'd followed the family profession?"

Her laugh was rich and intoxicating.

"Goodness me, no! I would have been terrible at it. I leave that to clever people like you. No, I knew from the first day I stepped into the Palace of Westminster that I'd done the right thing. Total joy. My home! Yes, don't laugh. It felt so homely."

"Well, you don't sound jaded about politics at all."

"I can be jaded about the Party, oh yes. Particularly now. Say what you like. But being an MP? Never. It is my calling. I will, God willing, keep doing it and serving my constituency until the day I die."

I felt many things: the warmth of her personality, mainly, but also a growing ease. I glanced across at Jay, chatting with colleagues we'd known for years, and felt that all I needed for the moment was there and at home. And then, when the time was right, I would emerge again and attempt the next step. In the meantime, nobody outside my family needed to know about my ambitions.

"So you don't think a life in politics is for you?"

"No," I said. "Well, maybe on a very small level. I wouldn't mind doing something useful, you know. Maybe some kind of voluntary work."

"Voluntary work," said Selma Henry, "is about the best thing any human can do. To give of yourself for nothing is invaluable to society. Volunteers are the truly good, the truly selfless."

"Well, I might just do that. I'm also going to spend as much time with my daughter as possible. She's doing A levels and is a bit needy, so I want to be there for her."

"Bravo!"

We talked a little more about children, about the constituency and some local issues and then we made the timeworn noises that signalled that we had reached the end of the conversation.

"Do come and see me whenever you want to," said Selma. "I could always do with a bit of advice, the way the party is going at the moment."

"Not sure how I can advise, but of course," I said.

"You want to know what the best feeling in the world is?" she asked me as she placed her glass on a shelf and turned to locate her handbag.

"Go on," I said.

She delivered a glorious smile. "Knowing the right place for you. And I agree, politics is probably not the right place for you. I can tell. But somewhere out there is the perfect role waiting for you and you have taken the first, brave step towards finding it. God bless you, my love."

I watched her go, that vivacious presence taking with it some of the light of the building as she left. Even if hadn't been nursing doubts, she would have instilled them, merely by setting such an impossible template. I wasn't a Selma Henry. She was a genuinely good person.

And yet . . . how often in my life so far had I been told I wasn't right for this or that? I'd never make it to such a good university, never get into journalism, never rise to the top. And now, someone taking a penetrating look at me and saying that, no, politics wasn't my natural fit. Forget it.

Only two people had truly believed in me and urged me onwards. One of them was now gone, had barely been there for a glorious second. And the other was dying.

3

DEIRDRA WAS IN hospital with a suspected stroke and there was a chance that they would have to remove a blood clot. Future strokes were, they said, inevitable.

Single for years, one of her children abroad, the other a bastard, she was now quite rightly my responsibility. I went to visit her every evening while she was in hospital. But the truth was that I was uncomfortable around this formerly mighty, now enfeebled woman. I couldn't bear to see her that way, with her sudden frailty and her new imperfections. I took Willa with me one night, partly to prise her out of her room, partly to give me a legitimate excuse to escape if things became unbearably sad.

Deirdra was happy to see us both but almost instantly closed in on herself. Her speech was slightly slurred and her brain a little foggy but she knew more or less who we were and what was what. She paused before each question as though having to construct them bit by bit in her head first.

"What story are you working on?" she asked me, as she always did.

I leant forward and touched her arm.

"Deirdra, I don't work there any more. I've left. Remember?"

She shook her head, searching for the information in her memory.

Willa, sitting beside me, smiled stoically but her fingers were all the while tapping on her phone.

"You haven't left, have you? *The Messenger?*"

"Yes, yes I have. That's right, *The Messenger.*"

"Best paper in the country, *The Messenger.*"

"Well . . ."

I wasn't going to discuss the much-of-a-muchness in British newspaper journalism with her at that point. I asked about the food and the friendliness of the nursing staff and she nodded and hummed distantly.

"We did everything we could . . .," she began.

I smiled, was patient. I owed her so much but I was poorly equipped to spectate on this slow extinction.

". . . to get you on that paper."

"I know," I reassured her. "And I'm grateful."

"You never know who can help you. You must reach out for help. Don't ever be shy."

"I know, Deirdra. You were amazing."

"What's happened to that awful boy?"

I glanced at Willa who suppressed a grin.

"That was years ago. I have no idea."

"He would have ruined your career. Everyone said so."

"Deirdra, really, you mustn't discuss my private life with other people, you know. It's weird."

She didn't have any fight any more, my aunt, and even this slightest, gentlest of remonstrations quelled something in her. Every time I saw her, those days, a little bit of her strength was sapped and her identity – or at least the person I knew her to be – diminished. I didn't know of a single sadder thing than the depletion of my Aunt Deirdra's character. Would it deplete me, too, to lose her? She had invested so much of her life in my own.

As we got up to leave – and every time I left her in the

days that followed – I worried that I might not see her again, that I might be leaving her *incorrectly*, botching our parting, fluffing my expression of the love that I felt for her and that I owed her.

"You take care, OK?" I said rather stupidly. Like these things were in her hands.

"I'm all right," she said, though it came out as a complaint.

As I retreated she held out a hand, surprising strong and steady. I returned to her side to hold it.

"Thank you," she said. "My lovely girl." She winked – extremely slowly and with some effort. "Thank you for letting me interfere in your life."

"Oh, Deirdra." I clung on hard so that nothing of the grief welling up inside me should be allowed to escape onto my face. "I still need you to keep interfering."

On the way home I told Willa: "Elderly people are absolutely obsessed with the distant past. They can't seem to focus on the now. Your grandma and grandpa are the same."

We were walking through the lamp-lit streets between the train station and our house. Willa always lagged behind me and I found it irritating to have to talk over my shoulder.

"Maybe the past is just more interesting," she said. "The past *is* interesting if you don't give a shit about the future."

My blood froze. My heart tripped. I remembered – I remembered that tone in another girl. It came back to me, that recklessness, that brazenness about life and death, nothing much mattering, the casual suggestion that the future can go fuck itself because she won't be there to see it.

I turned at once and blocked her path. She looked up from her phone, her eyes wide.

"Don't talk like that. Don't you dare talk like that!"

"What? What did I say?"

I was as surprised by my vehemence as she was. She was a little afraid, too, and trying to conceal it.

"The future is all yours. It's yours. It should excite you. It's full of possibilities."

She was embarrassed.

"All right. Whatever."

"No! Not all right. I don't want you to think like that."

"I think the way I think, Mum. You can't change that. I can't change that. Anyway, I was talking about Deirdra. What's your problem?"

But the maelstrom was not calming. I was being taken back, too far back, to a conversation that had never left me, that still haunted me. Maybe I had never escaped its logic, never moved beyond its perverse perfection of thought.

I couldn't leave it. I had to impress on my daughter how I felt. But she was finding it immensely awkward.

"I'm sorry," I told her. "It's just that I worry about your world view."

"My *world view*?"

"I mean, I want you to feel the excitement I felt at your age."

It was clear I had lost her. She was peering over my shoulder.

"I want you to look forward to things, that's all. Willa, please listen to me."

"What's going on there?" she said, side-stepping me and pointing to the end of the road.

I found it difficult to snap out of it, wasn't certain if this was some stalling tactic. I turned and saw a white van in the near distance. Its engine was running and it didn't take me too long to work out that its driver was removing the van's contents and piling them on the middle of the road.

"He's fly-tipping, Mum."

"What the hell!"

I broke out into a run at once, heading straight for him. When he saw me, he made for the driver's seat.

"Willa! Take a picture of the number plate. Now!"

As the van drove off, more of the rubbish – building materials, old kitchen cupboard doors, empty paint tins, the usual stuff – fell in a trail on the road behind him.

"The bastard. The total bastard. Come back!"

He was gone and my daughter and I stood in a small sea of rubble.

"I got the number plate," she told me, holding up her phone.

"Then we've got him," I said and it was as easy as that, mother and daughter united, any unpleasantness between us instantly smoothed over, a new impulse kicking in. And, though I barely knew it, another cog turning, its teeth fitting perfectly into place, the whole machine once more kicking in.

"You're my clever girl," I told her. "I'll show you what it means to have some purpose."

⁂

After the court case, I acquired a new reputation – as the scourge of fly-tippers.

The man Willa and I had caught that night in the process of emptying his van in the middle of a residential street turned out to have a record in environmental offences and our evidence was used to convict him. I hadn't wavered for a second in turning him in. Our home turf was typical of London, a social and economic mix, with – say what you like about the capital – a strong sense of community. People cared about any level of lawlessness and were frustrated to see criminals getting away with it. Waking up to a freshly abandoned mound of builder's waste was a depressingly regular event and we all felt impotent when it came to stopping it.

My family and I lived in a truncated terrace of thin, three-storey Georgian houses. Bounded on one side by rows and rows of classic Victorian homes and on the other by a vast 1970s housing estate, our little parade was like a page ripped from an old book. In the early days I hated the area, worried whether it was the right place to bring up my kids, feared that Jay and I would never leave it and grow old among the waves and waves of new, young, fearless urbanites. But then, over the years, I realised there were still delights to be had, rewards to be uncovered, in my neighbourhood. I simply needed to let myself love it. And I did, very much. Instead of upsetting myself that we might never leave it, I started to agonise over how I would ever separate myself from my home.

Now that I had time on my hands, I planned to renovate our house, bring in a little more light and beautify the garden. So, do up the garden and look after the daughter. That's a plan, isn't it? As good as any other.

But people kept coming and asking me to join things, to help rebuild a community garden, to sit on a health trust committee. The latter only took up a couple of days a month but it was just the right amount of commitment. And of course there was the local paper, which featured me on the cover several times as an "activist" and for whom I was a ready-made supplier of quotes and opinions – given that I knew how to play the game. None of it was too taxing. None of it took me away from Willa for long, and sometimes I even dragged her with me.

As the smaller commitments began to mount, Jay suggested that I should simply run as a local councillor and be done with it. Willa was amused that I didn't mind being associated with such parochial matters after having reported on the comings and goings of Westminster.

"Why are you farting around with dumped rubbish, Mum? Why not just be done with it and stand for Parliament? That's what you really want, face it."

My other two children, coming and going from their lives beyond us, were mildly interested in what I was up to. I loved it when we were all together, when Christmas came, and then when Christmas was over I struggled with the emptiness. I focused on getting Willa to study properly, set her timetables and bought her revision guides. She wanted me beside her all the time, so I often sat on one end of her bed working away on my laptop while she sat at the other end doing the same on hers. Under the yellow glow of her bedside lamp, we sat together, two friends, two students, individually occupied, but conjoined in the peace and neutrality of a teenage girl's bedroom.

As the Spring approached, and with it her mock A levels, we were a tightly-bound, exam-conquering team. More than once, she suggested that I come into the exam hall with her and sit quietly facing her. It was only a half-joke, I suspect.

She passed them relatively well and we promised each other we'd redouble our efforts for the real thing. I don't think my mind was trained on those A Levels any less sharply than hers. She wanted to go to my old university and, given that it was a very good university, I encouraged her to try.

I worked on the garden, re-painted the house, studied with Willa in the evenings, attended health trust meetings, fielded fly-tipping complaints to the council, and didn't notice how bored I'd become and how restless. Didn't know how ready I was for someone to enter my life and stir things up once more.

4

I TOOK WILLA with me to my old flat.

I drove because we had cleaning materials with us. It was July and very warm and we were in T-shirts and shorts and we carried buckets and sponges and cleaning products up the three flights of stairs.

"God, you went up and down all these stairs every day," she marvelled.

"They're only stairs," I said, and hovered on the landing where my friends Abi and Kate had lived. They were long gone now and there had been no goodbyes. Things just moved on.

I'd been unhappy with the letting agents of late and decided to take charge of renting out the flat myself. Willa and I would clean it, furnish it and get it ready for the new tenants. I had time, after all, to handle the administration of being a landlord.

My daughter wasn't the most assiduous of cleaners but then neither was I at her age. Cleaning is just one of those domestic skills you have no choice but to pick up. She was better at going on errands, running down to the WH Smiths by the station for cold drinks or to the hardware shop for more multi-surface cleaner.

The last tenant had been less than hygienic, and I had to remove embedded grime from kitchen corners and behind the loo. Meanwhile, Willa swept and dusted and listened to her music.

"Did you like living here, Mum?" she called out from the bedroom.

"Loved it," I answered, from the bathroom, but even as I said it, I was removing certain unwanted images from my memory.

She came to the bathroom door and watched me. Her satin brown hair, fluid and heavy, was caught in a high ponytail.

"Will I ever be able to live in a place like this?"

"Why not? It's yours whenever you want it."

She was inspecting the walls, making calculations.

"At least, if I live here, I'll still be close to you."

I got up off my knees.

"Listen. After one year of university, you'll be so stuck on your new life, the last thing you'll want is to be anywhere near me."

"That's not what I meant," she said, and followed me to the kitchen. "I meant that this place kind of reminds me of you. It's got you all over it."

It's just a space, I thought to myself. *Don't imbue it with anything.*

I picked her chin up in my hand.

"Everything will be fine. I promise."

A new bed was delivered pretty much on time and we unwrapped the bedlinen we'd bought and aired the new duvet. We had china and cutlery and placed them in the kitchen drawers and cupboards. The sofa in the living room was relatively new and unstained but I put a new loose cover on it just for the sake of change. The walls remained bare, the furniture and décor minimal.

How undemanding and simple a space. A person could just exist here. Endure for a while. How desirable the blankness of it seemed to me. And, I think, to my daughter. After I had checked and tuned the telly and made sure the sockets were functioning, I went to find her on the bed.

"Oi! Get off. That's meant to be pristine for the new tenant."

She started rolling about and clowning like a five-year-old. I sat down beside her and tried to clamp down her legs to stop her. We were both laughing and enjoying ourselves.

Oh God. Why must it end!

I love you. I don't want you to leave me any more than you want to leave.

"Get up, oaf," I told her.

We straightened the bed with meticulous care and left the building as the evening sun slanted in and floodlit every cauterised inch of that stainless flat.

༺❀༻

The potential new tenant was due at 11am the following day. We drove through clear sunny streets to arrive half an hour in advance and I carried up a few items I'd forgotten the day before, namely a saucepan and a replacement shower curtain.

The meeting had been arranged via email and our visitor was called Vivek Batra.

At eleven the intercom bell buzzed and I pushed the button and opened the door.

Willa pulled a face of excessive horror at me and disappeared into the bedroom.

I opened the door not to a man, but to a woman. And not an Indian woman, either.

She looked at me and smiled. I needed a moment or two.

Of course, it was. Of course.

"No way!" I said.

She stepped inside the flat with a huge smile and wide-open arms.

Avril explained to me that she was there on behalf of a colleague.

I couldn't take my eyes off her. She was gorgeous. She'd started blooming when I last saw her twenty years ago, an easy-going teenager, wise beyond her years, waiting for her moment, astute, careful. I visited a girl in her council-run home, living in cheap tracksuits and grateful for anything she got. And now there was no more waiting for her. Standing in front of me was an elegant, worldly working woman in her late thirties. Her hair was cut very short, hugged her skull, and suited her well-proportioned features. Her smile, in particular, was arresting. Broad, healthy, positive. She was in a red shirt dress and red patent heels, the simple pairing giving a strong account of her energy and confidence.

She was one of a team of in-house lawyers based at a large, international shipping company, she told me. Occasionally she would be called upon to check out apartments for senior managers and partners who needed a short let.

"Out here!" I exclaimed. "Surely you'd put them up in Knightsbridge or something."

"This would suit Vivek right down to the ground. He doesn't want to be in Knightsbridge or something."

"Well OK. You know best."

I asked her to come and sit down – I was so pleased to see

164

her again – and we settled on the new sofa cover and grinned at each other.

"You did it," I told her breathlessly. "The career, everything."

"Yeah, I guess I did." Her refined accent was warmed through with a hint of South London. "Turns out I love corporate life. It's all about sorting things out and making good. There's a very real pleasure in making things happen for other people."

She had two young boys under ten. Their father was also a lawyer – called Sean – and they lived in a newbuild apartment by the river in Greenwich.

"You got your man," she told me. "I can't tell you how relieved I was that it all worked out. You'd been unhappy for so long."

Of course she'd known this at the time, because I wrote to her now and again in her first year at university, revealing only the most pertinent – and positive - details of my life.

"Yes and three kids. Place in Deptford – not far from you at all as it turns out. Bit of an old wreck but I'm slowly doing it up."

"And the dream job is over."

"You're *very* well informed," I said.

"I *consume* news. Your byline disappeared. I guessed you'd moved on."

"Actually" I said. "I've got one of my brood here at the moment. My youngest."

"You have? Excellent," and she clapped her hands.

I called Willa over. My daughter came a little sullenly and shyly into the living room. Avril asked her age.

"Eighteen? I was the same age when your mum came to

help me with my studies. Oh my God, but I owe her so much."

"No," I demurred. "I owe *you*. You were the bright point of a difficult time for me. I used to hang around Renfrew House so I didn't have to go home."

"Still, that's old history, isn't it?" she said. "Those difficult times."

There was something so upbeat and business-like and reassuring about her. I didn't want to let her go, even though she told me that she had to get back to the office at Canary Wharf.

We did a quick tour of the flat and she seemed happy with everything she saw. I watched her as she casually examined the fixtures and fittings. How blissful it felt to know that she was leading such a fulfilled and successful life. Although reflecting on another's success can, in people like me, bring with it a moment of morbidity.

Was I going to start looking back soon, rather than forward?

No. It was her moment now, not mine.

"Better get on," she said and made her way to the door.

"We mustn't lose touch," I said.

"We won't."

"Avril, you *are* happy, aren't you?"

She made a clicking sound. A sighing. Accompanied by an expansive, exultant gesture. There was so much going on in those buoyant features.

"I would've been happy with half of what I've got," she said.

I'm sure she didn't want me to, but I felt ashamed of myself.

I found Willa sprawled on the bed.

As she lay there, I positioned myself by the little round bedroom window with my back to her and let my eyes drift across the deceptively green vista of South East London, from Sydenham, through the ups and downs of the outlying boroughs of Bromley and Bexley, out towards the fringes of North Kent, the suburbs, Hayes, Elmers End; to the east Dartford and the places I knew to be intersected by major roads, heavy with lorries, sided by industry. But from where I was, it was positively arcadian, spires and rooftops, chimneys and high-rises, all sinking beneath a froth of treetops, parks and woodland.

"She's nice," I heard my daughter say.

"She really is."

It was warm in the bedroom and I fiddled with the latch of the window and managed to get it open. The new air brought with it the sounds of dogs and children, of sirens and the miles-away thrum of freight trains, and birdsong. Of a mere slice of a vast and complex city, in other words.

"Mum?"

I turned to find Willa sitting on the side of the bed, her face creased in thought.

"Someone slept on this bed last night."

It often troubles me how hard I find it to follow my children's line of thought. When they are together and excited they flit from subject to subject at breakneck speed, ideas flashing vividly between them in a codified language known only to them and their age group. My first instinct is to swat away all the babble, try and make a stand for sense. I resort to authority.

I assumed I hadn't understood her.

"No," I said. "No one did."

"Yes," she insisted. "I'm sure of it."

I was already losing patience. Why? Why didn't I simply believe her?

"It's impossible," I told her. "Only I hold the keys now. No one else can come in here. Anyway, the bed looks exactly the same as when we left it."

That face tipped up to mine. Concerned.

"It doesn't *smell* the same, or *feel* the same."

"Willa."

"I could tell straight away. I was the last to see the duvet last night and it was different this morning. Like it had been used and quickly put right. And I can *smell* that someone was here."

Willa's sense of smell was legendary in our house, but all the same . . .

"It's not possible, darling."

"It's perfectly possible."

"We're going."

I wanted to change the subject, didn't want her imagination to run wild.

I couldn't express to her my own neck-prickling feeling that morning as I stepped into my old flat that something was different about it, some addition, some visitation, something concealed and uncanny. It had made me shiver and succumb.

5

I T WAS AVRIL who suggested that I take the next step and stand for a parliamentary seat.

Half a year had passed since the reunion in my flat and a friendship had grown up between us. To be precise, it had sprung anew. It had never been a close relationship before as such, because we had been too conscious of our age and life-stage differences. But now we were two adult women in that neurotic rush of middle life, experiencing our ageing through the growth of our children and the ebb and flow of our careers.

Jay and I were invited to dinner at the riverside flat and we had found an immaculate home, a likeable husband and two bright and engaging little boys. I remember we walked back from that dinner and there had been an astonishingly huge sunset, people stopping on the Thames footpath to take their pictures against the orange sky.

"Avril's boys are lovely," I told him absently.

"Weren't they great?"

I turned to him.

"This is not an end, you know. Just because ours have left home. We're not just going to be grandparents and our lives aren't going to dribble away to nothing."

He seemed astonished. "Woah. Where's that come from? Grandparents!"

I was suffering. Willa had started university and her departure left a surprisingly vast space. Jay and I had planned so many trips and adventures for when we were alone again but now the time had come, I was restless and uneasy, waiting for my girl to come home. Waiting, often, for a call from her that she wanted me with her, to watch over her.

"You're bored, aren't you?" he said.

"I'm not bored. I'm not. I'm just a little uncertain. I feel oddly unguided."

"I miss her, too," he told me.

Did I even listen? *Have I listened enough to you? Have you always known?*

We came back to an empty house and a sudden call from Avril.

"I've been thinking about our conversation over dinner," she said. "This is mad, but you've got to go for it. This is the perfect moment for you to take the next step. Come on!"

How compelling – how hypnotising – to be believed in this much!

"The Party needs new blood. Things have to change and be shaken up. He won't be leading it for ever and when he goes it will take a long time for them to convince people to vote for them again. Listen, I don't live and breathe politics, like you. I get off on making things happen. What do you say?"

I didn't know what to say.

"I know for a fact that you're making an impression on people. I read all the papers, remember. You're not afraid to deal with the small stuff. People admire you. You're a local mother who, in her own small way, makes a difference."

"Oh please."

"You are the kind of person that the Party needs to re-connect to the public."

"The public connects very happily with Selma."

Which is where she faltered and went silent.

"What are you suggesting?" I asked her.

"You gotta replace her."

I had to think for a moment.

"Selma?"

"Yes, Selma."

Now this *was* funny.

"You're out of your mind. Why on earth would anyone even dream of replacing Selma? Anyway, she's not stepping down. Oh and why are *you* getting so excited over this?"

I could hear the passion from the other side. It came as a total surprise to me – none of it had surfaced over dinner. It was almost like she'd taken advice since I left. Or just felt inspired while digesting our dinner party talk.

"Let me be your campaign manager," she cried. "Oh please. I've always wanted to do something like that. I'm very good at strategic thinking. And my employer would have no problem. Please!"

What could I say? In the last couple of months I had been increasing my local voluntary activity and I knew I'd reached a crossroads. But was now the time to step it up? Was it that easy? Could the moment a young girl decided 35-odd years ago to "do good" just lurch back into life?

"Sure," I said, uncertain of what I was really committing myself to. "But we leave Selma alone. We enquire about seats coming free elsewhere. OK?"

"Let's do this!" she exclaimed.

Let's do this. Let's complete the plan.

"OK," I said. "Welcome to a campaign I didn't even know was happening!"

I was running down the steps, round and round, floor after floor, and all I could see was the hem of a dress disappearing round each corner. I couldn't keep up and my heart was pounding. I had been put in charge – she was my responsibility – but I was flailing, way behind, in eternal panic.

I couldn't keep up.

6

E VENTS. IS THAT all I can give you? I'm sorry if they make little sense. But you must understand I'm on this journey with you at exactly the same time as you. As you read these events, so do I. As you try and grasp their relevance, so do I.

They're not even the events that I would rather tell you about, the ordinary, the routine, the daily unpacking of love and life that occurs in a growing family. The terrible compact you make with another person: the more you grow to love him, the less time you have together. I know these things are beautiful, but they weigh heavily, too.

Why do I always feel their impermanence? Is it just my nature? It's some execrable fucking curse. I can't – I *can't* – believe in myself. Why can't I have the faith in myself that others seem to have in me?

The ground is continually shaking beneath my feet and until I remember everything – every single moment that might have been relevant – I can't even begin to lead my proper, my naturally, healthily ebbing life.

But these events all lean on each other and when one falls the others fall as well. That's all I can say. The rest we must learn together.

The young reporter came to call on me at six and we set off in my car to an industrial estate near the main railway line that ran into London Bridge.

Jay wasn't home from work. Willa was in her first term at university. I told the dog I was leaving him in charge when I left home.

The sky had been cloudy all day and it would be dark early, maybe in the next hour. When we arrived at the entrance to the estate, its distant depths were already cast in shadow. The reporter, who was called Megan, and who was nowhere near as excited as I was, got out of the car to get her bearings.

"I'm told it's the lane down behind the units. There's an area where the fence has been broken through."

"OK," I said, getting out and beeping the car door shut. "Let's go and have a look."

We both had torches and were alert and ready. I'd expected a photographer to come with us but Megan said the reporters took all the pictures themselves these days. I wanted to ask her about newsroom life and maybe tell her a bit about my early days in the trade, but I felt we ought to be quiet. The estate was owned by a private company and remained open all night, many of the businesses based there being hauliers who came and went at all hours. We hadn't asked for permission to be on the site but then neither had the fly-tippers. The landlords either turned a blind eye to the illegal dumping and expected the council to clear it up or were genuinely caught out by the perpetrators. Anyway, that's what we were here to assess. It was Megan who had been told about it and she had come straight to me.

We agreed that we would sit it out for two hours max. If no one showed up then we'd go away and come back another day.

"Proper investigative journalism, this," I told her, with a tone similar to the one I used to rally my three when they were little.

"Yeah," she replied, drily.

Megan was slight, well-spoken, and swamped in a fleece. She didn't seem confident enough in our working relationship to exhibit any humour or lightness. But I was loving every minute. It made me feel very young – to be hunting wrong-doers. I felt like I was playing. When had I last played? Never. I worked. Always. Even as an adolescent I was studying too hard to let myself go. And then I needed to recover before I started the onslaught all over again. Let me play. Let me do something daft and rather unseemly and totally inappropriate for my age. Let life just take me on this puerile adventure. Who did I have to answer to? No one but myself.

We came to the fence that ran along the back of the property parallel with the railway line and followed it to the outer perimeter of the estate. Opposite us were the great, dark hollows of the industrial units and warehouses. Near the entrance they had been modern and unremarkable but, this far in, the storage spaces were clearly older buildings, made of brick and with huge wooden gates rather the metal shutters.

Most of them were locked for the night. In a very few the lights were still glowing. Occasionally we heard the crash of goods being loaded, or the shuddering rush of a shutter coming down.

"Ah, this is it," announced my companion and pointed to a large section of the fence that was missing. Moving closer, we saw that the area beyond it was paved, once a courtyard or loading area when the site was first used at the turn of the last century. Maybe even part of an old stable block. But it was

nothing more than a large skip now. Everywhere were flut-
tering, mouldering piles of trash: bags of old clothes, broken
garden furniture, window frames, splintered brooms, sodden
cardboard, and mattresses of course. All the detritus of domestic life that people had paid to get out from under their
feet, assuming it would end up in a legitimate dump.

"The utter bastards," I said.

"It stinks," said Megan.

"So, now we just wait, do we?" I asked.

Megan was the lead here. She was the one who had been
told about the site. She was the one who would write the story.
I was just fact-finding.

"Yeah, let's give it an hour, tops. I'm hoping to go out
tonight."

I agreed. An hour was enough for me, too. If no vans
arrived in that time I'd at least know where to come back.

"This is so much better than political reporting," I told her.

"Is it?" she replied flatly.

"It's all talk, politics, you see. There's no *doing*."

"Really."

"You could spin a whole series of stories based on something someone said off the record about someone else. None
of it amounting to much. And then at the end of it, you'd
think: *did I just get excited about all that? It was a whole lot
of nothing.*"

"Goodness."

And it went on in that vein, me relishing the intrigue of
our mission, Megan checking her phone for the best bus routes
to the restaurant where she was meeting her friends. Often we
were silent. Tucked into the shadows of a vast storage unit,
the late spring night drawing in, we managed somehow to get

through an hour and ten minutes before looking at each other at exactly the same time.

"Shall we knock it on the head?" she asked.

"Seems a shame to give up already," I tried.

But she wasn't having it.

"I would say stay without me, but I need a lift."

I looked around one last time, told myself I would be back one day soon, and waited while she checked her phone once again.

"That's funny," she said, frowning at the screen.

It was dark by now and her face was underlit by the phone screen. I heard her muttering to herself.

"What?" I asked.

"It just says *unit 12, side door.*"

"What does?"

"A message. I don't recognise the number. Just *unit 12, side door.*"

"Now then, Megan, that sounds like a tip-off to me."

She slumped and her voice became a whine.

"But I'm going out tonight."

"Just a quick look."

We clicked our torches on. The beams chased around the brickwork of the wall beside me and revealed a wooden plaque with the number 11.

"Over here, it's the next one," I called, already on my way. We were heading to the furthest reaches of the industrial estate – to a warehouse that stood in silent blackness against a similar sky. When we got to it, it seemed enormous, storeys high.

"Where's the side door?" I asked.

"The side, perhaps."

I was beginning to wish I was on my own. This girl wasn't enjoying the chase.

"What are we looking for anyway?" she asked, following me to the corner.

"We will oblige your source by checking out whatever is in the warehouse and then returning home."

"God," she muttered under her breath. Where's the stamina these days, I asked myself, as I searched for the side door.

I found it. A wooden gate so far down the side of the building that we had been on the point of giving up and looking elsewhere. I reached out and pushed it. It opened easily.

"Wonder why it's not locked," said Megan.

"I was thinking exactly the same thing."

Inside, the warehouse stank of decay and damp and neglect. But there was a much stronger stench overlaying all that: burnt plastic. It was so strong that I felt it scour my throat and retched to get it out. I trained the torch against the inner wall until I located a large switch and pressed it.

The light revealed a puzzling sight. I couldn't quite grasp what it all was at first because it seemed so innocuous. Just more rubbish. When I say more, I mean, tons and tons of it, mountainous, piled high into the rafters of a warehouse that must have been around 30 feet tall. And then I realised what I was looking at. I was looking at fraud.

"Megan, you know what this is?"

"More shit."

"Yes, but look at that!"

I was pointing to a brick furnace situated directly opposite us against the far wall, its mouth blackened from excessive use. A flue ran from the top and out through the wall into the side alley. It wasn't a huge structure. Burning anything in it would have to be done bit by bit, batch by batch.

"I don't understand," she said.

I waved my arm towards the mounds of plastic all around us: mainly bottles but also tubs and containers of all sizes. Hundreds of thousands of pieces of plastic.

"Why is this here?" I wanted to know. "It shouldn't be. We pay the council to collect our recycling and to . . . well, to recycle it."

"Well, aren't they recycling it here?"

"Oh Megan! Look at it. It's dumped. It's been here for ages. Someone collected this and just lobbed it here and – judging by that appalling acrid smell – is illegally burning it. I know all the recycling sites in our area and this isn't one of them. And anyway, why would someone tip us off if it wasn't untoward?"

"The fuckers," she said.

"Exactly."

But she wasn't as impressed with our discovery as I felt she ought to be.

"Great," she drawled. "So this is the big scoop? Plastic bottles?"

"Don't you understand?" She really was the most exasperating reporter. At least I'd never been this dense. "We are all paying our taxes for this stuff to be collected, sorted and recycled. Instead, someone is bringing it here and hiding it – and pocketing a shedload of council money. And judging by the amount of fox shit, several generations have happily reared their cubs undisturbed in here. This is a crime. These people are scum. Probably very well-paid scum."

"Hang on," she said and took out her phone. Before I knew what was happening, she'd taken a picture of me standing beside the rank mountain of plastic. "OK," she said. "Leave it with me."

"Christ," I muttered, surveying the foul-smelling scene. "Who can you trust, eh?"

"Is someone here?" she suddenly asked.

I spun around. There was no one but she'd set my heart speeding. I was on the point of telling her off.

"Sorry," she said. "I thought I heard feet, outside the door."

I crossed the concrete floor and stood by the door and waited, not entirely comfortable with opening it and looking out.

"Can we just go?" I heard her say.

I reached out and opened the door.

⁂

What do I remember? Think. *Think.* I see things so differently now that it's almost impossible to return to that place, that night, and to recall exactly what I witnessed.

I know the air was cool and that I shivered. I know the sky was low and inky and that we were so small among these great dark buildings, so exposed. Was I afraid? No, I don't think I was. I'd been playing and I was open to anything, a little befuddled, but going along with it. I was proud of myself, for once, because I'd taken the initiative and worked something out. I was having my adventure. I never stopped to think what led me there or why it had all been so easy.

I never stopped to think at all.

And was there someone there? Yes, it was someone who, when he or she saw me, stepped back into the shadow of a warehouse and disappeared. I couldn't identify that person in the gloom. But I can now. *Then*, I assumed it was a security guard or an employee. Now, I know it wasn't.

⁂

So, was that the adventure? Does it warrant the telling – two women coming across a warehouse of abandoned plastic bottles, ready meal cartons and fruit punnets? Why should I go out of my way to tell you about the discovery of a hundred thousand bottles in a dark, dank hole?

Who cares? Yes, it was a crime and a travesty of trust, but how many other crimes were being committed in that industrial estate that night? Plenty, I'm sure. Small, grubby abuses and petty violations. I wasn't a police officer. I wasn't a judge. Why should I care?

Why on earth should *you* care?

No, the story is nothing. The crime is unglamorous. The sense of anger dissipates very soon. It's all rubbish, after all. Who can get too worked up about it?

But you need to know and I need to tell.

What had started was not yet finished.

7

WILLA CALLED ME in tears and asked if she could come home. This wasn't the first such call since she'd left but that didn't make it any easier. Avril was coming round soon and I was cooking. My daughter was trying my patience and my nerves were raw.

Several saucepans were on the go at the same time and I paced about the kitchen with the phone to my ear.

All I remember is my exasperation with her, my it'll-get-better incantation. It simply fanned things.

"Mum, *please*," she pleaded. "I don't like it. I can't cope."

"This isn't school, sweetheart. You can't just up and walk out. Anyway, what about your loan?"

What a reprehensible game to play with your own suffering child. I wanted her off the phone. I wanted this drawn-out melodrama to stop. I wasn't being kind or at all good.

I'd run with open arms to university. I loved it and looked on as others behaved in a flaky, trying way. But she was my child. She didn't have to be me. If she was flaky and trying then I was the one who should adapt.

I knew what she wanted. She wanted me there with her. It was the only way she would get through and start to grow up.

"I have to go, darling," I told her. "I'm expecting Avril. Call your sister right now. She'll calm you down a bit."

The water was boiling and ready for the pasta. The

doorbell rang. We said our goodbyes and I rushed along the hall to let Avril in.

"Evening," she called, stepping in and removing her phone from her bag. "Seen the *News Shopper*? You're in their lead story."

I couldn't even muster a response. Featuring in the local paper had ceased to be a cause of excitement. It was nearly always the same thing anyway: a picture of an old mattress and a headshot of me with a cut-out quote about anti-social behaviour.

Avril arrived in the kitchen and held out her phone.

"Nice one," she said.

I had two pots on the go and couldn't leave them.

"What's the headline?"

She read aloud: "Local MP implicated in recycling scandal."

I formed the word *what* but didn't hear it come out. The saucepans were bubbling.

She carried on: "Branded scum by activist".

My voice, when it finally arrived, was faint. I sounded like someone who had been punched in the throat.

"May I see?"

The saucepans simmered. It was all you could hear.

I read the article through – it was short and clumsy – and looked at Avril and she looked back at me.

Under Megan's by-line was a story that came as a surprise. I mean, the fact of it appearing. No one had warned me or told me I was going to be quoted. No one called me up – as I would have done – and asked for my reaction to a stunning discovery. And what was that discovery? Pretty much as I had divined: that the council paid a company five years ago to collect a surplus of domestic waste plastic; to sort it, clean it, and take it to be recycled. It was a one-off contract worth around £120,000, arranged under the radar. But the company had pocketed the money and dumped the waste in a secure warehouse, even burning some of it to make space. Utterly brazen, astonishingly despicable, totally idiotic given that these things are monitored, because a council has to be accountable for the spending of public money.

And the company? Well, this is why my voice failed me and why I stood mutely as my cooking pots spat angrily beside me. It was called The Birdsong Company and it was owned by a man called Mike Henry. And Mike Henry was married to Selma Henry MP. And Selma Henry MP and her husband were close family friends of the chair of the council's environment committee. A quite staggering double-whammy of cronyism and corruption on the one side and bare-faced criminal activity on the other. And all of it conveniently brushed over and forgotten about.

"You've scored a blinder there," I heard Avril say.

"I didn't do this," I told her, still staggered. "I don't even believe it."

"I do!"

Accompanying this breathless exposé was a picture of me standing beside a teetering monument to polyethylene tere-phthalate. The heroine. Front and centre. Deeply satisfied with her work. *Activist and local mum.* I ask you – who wouldn't admire such a public-spirited figure? And how good she is. How very, very good. What's the point of doing anything good anyway if no one knows you're doing it? Let's applaud her. Let's keep her going on this lifelong quest to do good for the world.

That's not me, I thought to myself. *That's just not me.*

Selma's fall from grace came astonishingly quickly. The Bird-song Scandal, as it became known, was rarely out of the local media, was mentioned once or twice nationally and featured as an on-going farce in *Private Eye*. A campaign by other parties in the constituency to get her ousted whipped itself up almost immediately. I felt sickened by it. Yes, Selma was a loyal Party member, but she'd never really played party politics. That was one of the many reasons she had been such an effective representative.

Avril warned me against communicating with her, said I should not stain myself by association. But I sent Selma an email telling her how sorry I was about everything and that I hoped she could ride it out. She never replied.

Avril sprang into action now, making the most of increased interest in me in the Party, both locally and nationally. It was extraordinary how quickly she made contacts and built bridges. I was worried for her job – she was spending so much time on me – but she said it had been sanctioned and was part of her "career growth".

There was a rumour that Selma was going to announce her resignation and that it would trigger a by-election. In fact, the new Prime Minister got there first, calling a general election, saying it was vital for strong and stable government.

"This is our moment," said Avril. "Are you ready to jump?"

Jay was there, I remember, and Avril's husband, Sean. We were in an Indian restaurant in Bermondsey. I looked from face to face and wondered what they really thought of me. Yes, even Jay. I was being put forward for selection as a member of Parliament to replace someone who seemed untouchable and I should have been emanating courage and confidence. Instead, I was letting it happen to me, looking to others to tell me where to put each foot.

When we were nearly home, I asked Jay: "Is this the right thing?"

"For you? Me? Or the country?"

"Any of the above."

Our common language, humorous and familiar, made up of light and loving mockery, seemed suddenly to fall short of everything we needed to say. I sensed that he was as uncomfortable.

"Then I'd say it's absolutely right for the country. You're not the usual *type* who goes up for this kind of thing. But it's not about what I think."

"It is," I said.

"Is it?" he asked and I felt the faintest draught of resentment. It made the hairs rise on my arms.

"I want to know what you really think."

"I think that you've always wanted this."

"Then . . ."

We were on the front step. He put his key in the lock but didn't turn it. Just stood, his shoulders dropped low, his face turned to the ground.

"Then why don't either of us feel overjoyed?" I asked him.

"I know why I don't."

"Why?"

"It's the timing, isn't it?" he said quietly.

I reached across him and finished opening the door and we went went inside.

He still couldn't quite look at me.

"We used to talk about this moment, in the pub, do you remember?"

I took off my coat, kept my back to him.

"Yes," I said.

"I used to think I'd do anything to help you. I was excited for you."

"Aren't you excited, now?"

He was slinging his coat onto the bannister. His expression was that vulnerable one, when he knew difficult things had to be said. For all his bluster and occasional storminess, he was never the disciplinarian with the kids. I was the one who had to be, on occasion, hated and pushed against.

"I'm going to run you a bath," he said, putting a foot on the bottom stair.

"I don't want a bath."

I wanted to know and I didn't. It was up to him to finish the idea and I would give him time but he had to say it.

"I'm very proud of you," he said.

"Just tell me."

"I don't think I should be saying this to you," he said. "It's not part of the plan. But . . ."

"But what?"

But what! If I haven't got you then I can't do this.

"I think it's great for the country if you're selected and if you stand. But I think it will be disastrous for our daughter."

Someone who is there for everyone. Who can help and be relied upon. A useful, dependable kind of person. I want to be good. I want to do something good.

But what does good even mean?

8

I STOOD ON the stage and I heard my name. I squinted at the crowd in front of me until I saw Jay and I smiled hopefully at him, though what I hoped for I don't know. Forgiveness? Understanding? And the returning officer read out the numbers and even in my tired, elated, horrified state, I didn't need to think. The gap between me and my nearest rival was in the many thousands.

I heard my name again, and I lifted my hand and there was an eruption of noise. People cheering me. People who didn't know me, exultant. People with a stake in me.

And I knew at that moment what I'd been suffering from all my life. It was suddenly clear to me.

From school to university to work to motherhood to political career. They had the wrong woman. I was a sham and sooner or later they'd all find out. How on earth could I carry on, a fraud? How could I convince everyone else when the only person who ought to have been sure of my rightness – me – had no confidence in it at all?

It was the mother of all imposter syndromes.

And it wasn't even a syndrome. It was a matter of fact.

Thank you.

Thank you so much to all of you who voted for me. I am deeply grateful that you have put your trust in someone unknown and untested.

All I want to say is this. And it goes out to everybody in this wonderful, vibrant, busy, life-affirming constituency of ours. Everybody.

I don't want to waste your time. I don't want to waste my time.

I don't want to be angry. I don't want to be part of a machine. I don't want to be known as an idealogue, as a party animal, as someone who follows a line. I don't care about what came before. I'm not interested in heritage. I don't want to be remembered as someone clever or indeed Machiavellian. I don't want to be labelled as someone to the left, centre or right of the party.

I just want to make things happen. I want to use the privilege of this position – of this rare moment of empowerment – to do something of use. I want, in short, to just get on with it.
And I want to thank the woman – an exceptional woman and most beloved friend to me – who has just died. We both dreamt of this moment a long time ago and to have achieved it without having her here with me right now is a great sadness to me.

Thank you.

9

"WHO? WHO'S JUST died?"

Avril was looking aghast.

"Didn't you like my speech?" I asked, blankly. "I thought you approved it." I'd been congratulated by a throng of people as I stepped off the stage. Avril pushed through to get to me and seemed panicked.

"I just want to know who you were talking about."

"My aunt," I said. "You knew she was ill. I told you."

"Your *aunt*?"

"She died three weeks ago. I definitely told you."

"Did you? OK."

We were swamped again. I couldn't bear to talk about Deirdra. Inside me was a maelstrom of grief, anger, fear and loneliness.

In the last few weeks, she hadn't understood what was going on immediately around her, let alone in my political career. I'd alternated canvassing with sitting by her side. Tess sat with her when I couldn't. I was moved by my oldest child's sense of responsibility and genuine compassion. She was doing it for me.

⁂

In the doorway at the back of the hall stood a man. Why he caught my eye in that bustling, neurotic, sleep-deprived crowd,

I don't know. His body language was different, I suppose, signalling neither brash victory nor bitter defeat. He was only there for a moment, peering round the frame. Even from that distance and in the mêlée around me, I could tell he was agitated and uncomfortable. He was tall and fair, and rather beautiful. Maybe that's why I noticed him.

Then I saw Avril walk up to him. She had been by my side only moments before. And now there she was, approaching this striking-looking man. She said barely a word or two to him before he nodded.

He looked at me briefly, and left the room.

❧

There was a party in the constituency office and then I went home to sleep in the afternoon, while Jay took calls and answered the emails of congratulation. Tess and Theo had come home for the vote. Willa had remained at university, even though term was ending. I felt like I'd been lifted up, shaken violently, put back down again and told to walk in a straight line.

I had to attend the celebratory dinner that night at a local restaurant. Also present were Jay, Tess, Theo, Avril and Sean. The mood was one of stunned disbelief on my part, reserved jubilation among the others.

At one point I turned to Avril and said:

"How will I ever square this with my family? It's going to tear me away from them."

She didn't even look up from her plate.

"Tear you away? I don't think women like us feel torn, really, do we?"

What had she got out of this, I wondered? Personal satisfaction? Extra attention from her employers? Sometimes I wondered if this was a test run for her own political ambitions. Or was it done out of friendship and loyalty to me? Oddly, the last of these possibilities convinced me the least. I wasn't sure if Avril wasted her considerable energies on something as fleeting as friendship.

That speech? It was an accurate reflection of my thinking, what there was of any sentience at the time. Avril had advised that the last thing I should do was to ally myself with any particular sect of a very sectarian party. There was going to be a bloodletting and I should put some blinkers on and walk straight through the centre of it.

Which was fair enough. I wasn't sure if I liked the Party very much any more.

"I'm tired," I told her. "More tired than I can remember."

Avril turned on her seat and rummaged for something in her handbag.

"I've been meaning to give you this."

She was holding a ticket.

"Tomorrow afternoon, you go off by yourself to the pictures. Right? When I get tired and can't take any more, it's my way of escaping. I switch off my phone, settle among all those strangers and just let it all play out in front of me. Absolute heaven. That's what films are for, aren't they!"

"I don't think I'll have time."

"Yes, you will. Surrey Quays Odeon. I'll drive you there myself. I've bought the ticket now. I don't want to waste it. Just . . . let yourself go."

It sounded both preposterous and rather enticing. But could I afford the time? Was it too profligate a use of an MP's day?

"Decided," she said, cutting my vacillations short, and returned to her meal.

❧

Don't ask me what the film was about. I slept through it. The minute the lights went down, my eyes closed. I remember liking the fact that the auditorium was largely empty when I arrived and then feeling aggrieved when people came in late and rustled and clicked and whispered around me. Did I really think I could have the place to myself!

No, I don't remember the film, but I remember the dream as though it had been a film. It was the same dream, the one where I forced myself to look over the windowsill and see Danielle lying on the grass far below me, mangled but happy, and free. Only this time, in a blink, I was down there beside her, on the dewy morning grass, and I was entwined in her limbs and hair, like they were part of an anatomical web. All the while I tried to break loose, we were smiling and laughing, tying ourselves into a tighter knot. And then my hand was on her face and she was closing her eyes and kissing my palm.

I felt like I was melting.

❧

The next two days were my own. To decompress, said Theo. Tess cooked for me, which was so touching. Jay called me from work every couple of hours to see how I was. It reminded me of those spare, shell-shocked hours after bringing a new baby back from the hospital.

Willa was painfully absent.

"Get your sister to come home," I told Tess. "She won't listen to me."

"I'm not sure she likes all the attention over here at the moment," she said.

"True. Then we'll leave her alone."

※

I started to emerge from the car crash that was my election. My new responsibilities weren't going to wait for me to pull myself together.

I was called to Portcullis House to be given an induction talk and assigned a buddy. All the enthusiasm was hushed, my new colleagues experiencing a mixture of pride and awe. We were told about the members' library, about the restaurants and the maiden speech. I listened as though I might have to pass the information on to somebody else.

The day after, I was to attend a lunchtime reception at party HQ. We had done monumentally badly in the election and the event was billed as more than a social gathering. It was meant to bring together everyone with a stake in reversing the decline: MPs, Peers, friendly media, donors, and high-profile supporters. I wasn't sure what I could bring to the table, given that I was so new, still swaying with the rapid change of direction in my life.

Jay offered to support me at the event but I had an urge to be alone. I wanted to walk through London for a while. It was early summer and I was nostalgic for something I'd only briefly known – relaxed, irresponsible youth. I wanted to look into shop windows and buy a Big Mac. I needed the neutrality of a department store and dawdled in the House of Fraser before taking things haltingly up Victoria Street.

Bit by bit I was beginning to leave behind my doubts and misgivings and convince myself that I wasn't being dragged along but was trudging by my own volition. With each passing flagstone, my feet felt lighter. By being alone I was remembering who I was. No one was guiding me or even shoving me. I had some say in my own life. The future was slightly alarming, but the present seemed to be settling in. If I took it day by day, if I didn't question how I'd got there, if I let myself act spontaneously and with humility and gratitude, well . . . maybe I could pull it off and survive this insane turnaround in my life.

As face after face passed me on the street, I began to feel once more like I was part of the mechanism, not the piece of grit that jammed it. I had some value. I had something important, perhaps, to contribute.

I remember, on that May morning, the grinding emergence of something like hope. I can recall every single small synaptic explosion of wonder with precision.

How? Because it was three days ago, and the last time I felt sure about anything.

PART FOUR

1

EVERY SINGLE PERSON at that reception spoke in the hushed tones of a conspirator. Clusters of people moved themselves aside as one and you knew it was because they were suddenly inspired to say something seditious. The undertone was one of theatrical muttering.

The whole room was frenetic with disloyalty or rather shifting loyalties. It caught – in sound and feeling – exactly what was so hateful about politics and yet so compelling. I saw faces I knew well, from TV or indeed from having interviewed them in the past, overwrought and with something manic working away at them from inside. Even the small new intake, of which I was a part, was impatient and not prepared to be side-lined. Had things to say.

As I walked into that room, I wanted to turn around and leave at once. I felt a strong sense of not being part of the club and not caring if the club didn't want me. But somehow I became absorbed into it, sucked into the hand-shaking, head-tipping vortex of necessary belonging.

My speech, my insistence that I wanted to set my sights to the side of party preferment, suddenly showed itself up to be laughably naïve. You couldn't do anything unless you understood how loyalties worked and unless you were prepared to gamble with your career.

Was this really where I thought I would start the process of changing the world? Had any of these people ever so deluded themselves as I had since childhood?

And dear God! Why would I want to change this world? I loved it. I loved its flaws and its tiny, microcosmic excitements. I loved the fact that it could go wrong at any moment. I loved our helplessness.

Did I care that much any more about the issues that sent me wild with rage as an adolescent? The so-called injustices? Could it be that all *that* was really all about me and not about the world at all? The world! What was I thinking!

I could have fallen to the ground there and then – my knees were buckling – and thumped the floor and declared everything a mistake, and I would have applauded them for carrying me away to a psychiatric ward. That's where I should have been. Not here, among these earnest career politicians, people who knew exactly what this job was about and had no illusions about their saintliness. They were pragmatic, hard-headed people, whatever their motivations. And I was the imposter.

Which was when I saw him again. Pale blue eyes trained directly in my direction. But only fleetingly and only before they were found out.

⁂

"Looks all wrong here, doesn't he," came a voice behind my right shoulder.

I turned and saw Caitlin.

It was no surprise to me that my former boss was at the event. As the editor of the Party's biggest media ally, it was unthinkable that she wouldn't be. The only surprise was that she should be anywhere near *me. The Messenger* had been the only paper to avoid coverage of the Birdsong Scandal. It had buried Selma's resignation among general election news. I assumed Caitlin would be hostile towards me, certainly not crossing a room to join me.

"Yes," I said, turning back to inspect him, finding sadly that he was no longer looking over at me. "He sticks out like a sore thumb in here."

"He sticks out like a sore thumb everywhere. D'you really not know who he is?"

I shook my head, feeling even smaller than before.

"That's Viggo Jespersen."

Something like recognition flickered in my brain.

"I don't know him."

"Ah, that's because he doesn't want us to know him. But we should, you know. He's rather important."

"Is he?"

Caitlin was amused and maybe a little drunk. Which came as a relief to me and explained a lot.

She leaned into me and tapped her nose with a hand that was already holding a wine glass. A drop of white wine landed on her powdered cheek.

"Major, major donor to the party. Very rich man. Stupidly rich."

I opened my mouth but she cut me off.

"Also, very publicity-shy. No one is supposed to know about his connections. The donations are made in the name of his family business."

"Right."

She stepped back and eyed me.

"You should know him though. You must have come across him while you were political editor."

"I don't think I did. No."

She swallowed some wine and said: "You're a strange one." Once again, I prepared to respond, only to be stopped. "One minute you're gushing over poor Selma Henry and telling her you've no political ambitions. The next you're sending her to the slaughterhouse and taking her job for yourself."

"That's not quite true, Caitlin."

"But that's what they're looking for, I suppose. Someone cut-throat. Well, you never know, you might help turn our fortunes around. Though I can't quite see it."

Oh, what was the point! I just wanted to get away from her, and surveyed the room to find someone who might rescue me. Avril was due a bit later; I could bide my time until then. But my eyes, as before, landed on him. What was it about him? He stood out physically, a good foot taller than everyone around him, his fair hair very youthful and Nordic, and his face otherworldly and politely refined. Well-bred. But there was something else. He was *removed*, that was it. Self-segregated. There seemed to be air between him and everyone else. He breathed different air.

"What are you looking at? Oh. Still him."

I didn't even turn to Caitlin. I didn't want to move from the sight of him to the sight of her. But when she spoke there was something softer there. Pity.

"I can't believe he's here today.

"Why not?" I asked.

Caitlin tipped her wine glass over to show it was empty and made a tragic face.

"Well, after what he's just been through. Right, I'm off to get a drink. Want something?"

I felt my phone vibrate in my bag and dug around to find

it. When I looked up, Caitlin had already moved off.

The hubbub was too much to answer a call, so I shouted a "hold on" down the line and moved out into the corridor.

❧

"I'm sorry," said the female voice, though it wasn't giving off any sense of apology, rather of susceptibility, as though she were doing something ill-advised. "We spoke many years ago. I don't suppose you'll even remember me."

"Who is this?"

"My name is Kim Gartner. You said you knew my sister. I was rather abrupt with you. Didn't quite trust your motives, I'm afraid. It was very rude of me. I've thought about it often since. My mother said that you did us an enormous service that night at the university with Danielle. I'm sorry."

I think she was deeply perplexed, despite being the instigator of the call. She wanted something from me and couldn't quite couch it correctly.

"Has something happened?" I asked.

Beyond the hall, the clamour from the guests spiked every now and again with a burst of laughter or a raised voice. I folded myself into a corner and pressed the phone to my ear.

"You have an expertise," she said.

"Have I?"

She had a gentle voice. It found the idea of having to impose on someone distasteful. She was suffering, I could tell that much.

"Yes, you understand the world a lot better than we do, I think. Your job means you have an ear to the ground. You know people. People tell you things."

"Oh goodness!" I exclaimed. "I'm afraid I don't do that any more. I haven't been a journalist for quite a while now."

"No?"

What a pitiful *no* it was.

"Then, I'm sorry."

I couldn't leave it like that. It wasn't about me, this call, so what did it matter what I did for a living?

"What do you want to know?" I pushed.

"It's not me, really. It's my mother. She'd just like to fill in the gaps. Then, I suppose you don't know that Danielle is now dead."

I wanted to say something but it was taking too long to work out what.

"We don't know when. We've just been informed about it. By her other family."

"What? What other family?"

Words, facts, were arriving at the surface of my mind. I wouldn't allow anything to sink deeper until later.

"She was married, apparently. It's remarkable that she kept that from us for so long. But this is the thing with people like her. They don't really care how much they upset people who love them. They're so inward-looking that the pain of others is . . . unimportant compared to the pain they themselves feel." And now her voice broke and so did everything inside me. "But she was our little sister and we've never understood or accepted why she disappeared out of our lives. We've tried to move on but . . ."

The words dropped slowly out of me.

"My God. How awful. How very, very awful."

An act of inhumanity was being described to me and

something in me – fear, a respect for bad luck – wanted to quickly box it up and put it aside.

"I can't imagine how much your poor parents must have suffered."

"My father died eight years ago. My mother is elderly but pretty sharp. She just wants to end all this, and to know."

The strain in my chest was almost unbearable. This was the body crying out when the voice couldn't.

"I'll find out what I can," I told her, hastily.

She remained silent. Possibly, she was too moved to speak.

"Do you know the name of her husband?"

"She kept it all from us, you see."

"I understand. But a name. Any details."

"My mother wrote it down. I can't remember. Oh God, I'm so stupid. Of course, it's important."

"It's all right, it's all right. Let me know when you find out. We'll take it from there."

"Thank you," she said. "I'll let you go. And I'm sorry. I'm sorry about being so unfriendly that time."

"It was a long time ago."

"So what do you do now? Now that you're not being a reporter?"

I honestly didn't know how to tell her. It sounded ludicrous to say: "Oh I've just become a member of Parliament." As though I had stepped from one unremarkable position to the other.

"Just between jobs," I told her.

In the long, self-conscious silence that followed, one of us eventually had the wit to ring off.

❧

An arm slipped through mine and I was was being dragged along.

"Come on, in we go. Let's face the music."

I glanced across at Avril and immediately relaxed in her care.

I'm sure she didn't want to be here any more than I did.

"What's the mood? Grim?"

I separated from her as we arrived at the door and moved back into the throng.

"Feels like it," I said.

I had been in there once already and thought I should be allowed to go home now. It felt a bit like arriving at a noisy playgroup with my mother. I didn't wish to leave Avril's side and I needed to find a way of convincing her to keep this short.

"Now listen," she said, sensing my drooping morale. "Let's get you introduced to as many people as possible. Election is one thing. Getting noticed by the right people is the real goal. I'll go get us drinks. I want to see you attached to at least one other person when I get back. Wish me luck. Just being seen next to a black woman is like getting a brownie badge to half of these fucking people."

As soon as she left, my mind returned to Danielle.

For years I had speculated on whether she was still here. And I felt convinced that she was. Not just here, but with me. How can I even begin to describe her presence? It was within me and around me. I interviewed a woman once who ran an African church in London. She told me that, for her, Christianity was not about God, or even Christ, but that less regarded member of the Trinity, the Holy Spirit. She had no time for God in the human form or even, surprisingly for

Bible stories. "It's all about the presence you feel around you. Inside you, outside you," she said. "It's supernatural."

I told her I didn't understand, but I thought of Danielle and the fact that somehow or other she had remained with me. Inside me, outside me. Supernatural.

Maybe all that had been my doing. She could have been dead for all those years, and yet I'd kept the precious treasure that was her locked up inside, unchanged. She was always there, nudging me out of lazy thinking and pushing me to ask questions. She gifted me her eccentricity and it was understood that I would carry it on in both our names.

I couldn't help thinking that I was never meant to know the reality of what happened to her and that, between us, her sister and I had transgressed and would pay a price.

The morning I woke up in her college room, my head numb, my face hot, I tried to understand what was going on by working my way out in concentric circles. Where on earth was I? Not, it suddenly came to me, where I should be: in my own bed. Slowly, Danielle came back to me, her dark curls falling over her eyes as she sat with her knees pulled up to her chin. I remembered the dress and the bare brown shoulder that slipped from the wide neckline.

Then I remembered our conversation and grew hotter with a moment of anger, thinking of how detached she'd seemed, what a dilettante, studying theology because it *interested* her. The world and its problems didn't matter to people like her, who looked inwards and didn't care about the beyond. And of course, that's when I allowed myself to remember why I was there in the first place. And it came with a jolt of panic. My eyes swept the room. I lifted myself onto my elbows. Nothing. I was alone.

And the window was wide open.

What had she said to me? When we were together on the bed, her hand on my ankle, what did she say? That she couldn't live another day? Was that it? She was telling me that it was unendurable, that she had an allergy to life. An allergy, for Christ's sake. In that vivid, merciless light, the air thickening, the torpidity already setting in, I was trying to cope with rising alarm and dread.

I got up and went to the window. I was acutely afraid – fear like I'd never known in my young life before. Was this moment about to leave a permanent scar?

I looked over the edge of the window at the ground, four floors down, and I saw grass. Untouched, shimmering in the intense light of another potentially unbearable day.

❧

Dr Waghorn was wearing a yellow floral dressing gown when she opened the door to me.

"You still here? Don't you have a home to go to?"

Once more she simply turned her back on me and left me to decide whether I should follow her inside or not. This time, I hovered in the doorway.

"But you asked me to keep watch over Danielle Gartner last night," I called after her. She stopped. "Danielle, the second year. The girl in danger of harming herself."

She looked about her at the papers and books on every seating space and I think she was relieved to see them instead of spaces that could be filled by living things.

"Oh yes," she sighed. "That go all right?"

What could I say? I fell asleep. My sole task had been to stay with her and keep her alive – a task I should never have been charged with, but things were different then, there were all sorts of gaps in responsibilities. Anyway, how could I tell this woman, who held my educational future in her palm, that I'd failed?

"I just wondered if you could tell me what happens next?"

I was making Dr Waghorn increasingly uncomfortable. I knew not to cross the threshold, but I couldn't go away either.

"That's her parents' business, not mine. I hear from the porter's lodge that they left at around 6am. I'm impressed you kept awake that long."

A weak smile from me. Nothing more.

"I doubt we'll see her again. I remember a similar case from a couple of years back. You get them, you know. Should never have come up in the first place. Look, if you're waiting for some kind of recognition, then . . . then thank you. I knew we could count on you and you came up with the goods."

"Oh no!" I was taken aback. "I don't want recognition."

I knew how irritated she was. This was all done with now. It was midday and heading into the afternoon and the un-pleasantness of the day before was long, long past.

"What will happen to her?"

Dr Waghorn scratched at an eyebrow and sighed so heavily that I found myself compelled to step back and away from her. I'd rarely felt such a strong force of repulsion.

"She'll either grow up or she'll go and do something stupid. Either way, there's nothing more we can do. Now, I suggest you go and put on some fresh clothes and go home to your family."

And this time when she turned her back on me I knew it was to signal that I should leave her alone and never mention Danielle's name to her again.

⁂

At the beginning of the new academic year, nearly three months later, I looked for Danielle's friends but was too timid to approach them. I didn't even know if they were her true friends – I just recalled seeing them with her. Time was passing and the college was forgetting her, but I couldn't get her out of my mind and didn't want to. Finally, on a wintry afternoon, having walked in the darkness by the river and felt myself aching with ignorance, I made my way to the common room where there was a women's welfare meeting going on. When it broke up, I approached the third-year who'd been conducting the meeting.

"Hi," I said.

"Hi." She was wearing some kind of squashed hat and a PLO scarf. "Did you get your pepper spray? We were handing them out at the start."

"I've got one," I told her and didn't wait to change the subject. "Can you help me with something?"

"Fire away," she said, placing her hands on her hips, ready for business.

"Do you know what happened to Danielle Gartner? I knew her a bit and just wondered if you'd heard any news."

The girl studied me a moment and her scowl suggested someone considering her options.

"She's left."

"I kind of guessed that."

"She's not coming back. We don't know much more than that."

"But her friends must have some news?"

"Maybe. I don't really think it was fair. But that's just my opinion."

"What do you mean?" I asked.

"Well, someone with serious problems needs proper help. I mean, she could have done something stupid and then a lot of people would have had to have dealt with that."

Stupid? It wasn't the right word. There was nothing whatsoever trivial or deficient about her thinking. I felt like I was an advocate for Danielle – that I would have to explain her.

"Are you feeling upset?" she wanted to know. "I can tell you the name of the welfare officer at the union if you want to talk about things. It's important to tell people how you feel."

And that bit of bland, scripted nonsense was all I could take. I didn't ask any more questions. I didn't want to hear some political diatribe about lack of government spending on mental health.

❧

She never went away.

When I sat in my flat and looked out of the window, she was sitting next to me.

When I came home in the bus, my head bumping against the rain-washed glass, she was on the other side, smiling back at me.

When I could take no more of Simon, she pushed me away from him. And when I yearned for Jay, she propelled me towards him.

She was there all the time and I knew that for her, wherever she was – *if* she still was – I was also there. What happened in that room that summer night had fixed us together. Because, despite our youth, we grappled with life and death in those early hours. We came close to nailing things that most people would far rather skirt around.

I had gloried in life, she had been comforted by death. It didn't matter. For each of us, that pure, perfect moment was where we began and ended. If it was love, then it wasn't like any love I'd ever read or heard about. It was a connection that sustained me.

She was, I felt, the *me* I couldn't quite see when I looked in the mirror.

2

A GLASS OF white wine was thrust in front of me, but it wasn't from Avril, who had clearly been grabbed just as she'd predicted, but from Caitlin, now visibly emboldened.

"All alone? That's not how it works. You're an MP. Should be schmoozing the room."

"I can't stay too long," I told her. "You were going to tell me something. About Viggo."

"First name terms, is it?"

I tried not to show the impatience and distaste I felt.

It wasn't the drink – but she looked tired. It was the pretence, I supposed. Having to be on top of everything always. Knowing everyone and everything that's going on. The price of remaining in journalism once the energy of youth has gone.

"You said he'd had a hard time."

She leant towards me.

"It's marvellous how much I find out. A gift. Wife died of cancer. Love of his life. He's in bits."

"How awful," I said.

"Hideous. Anyway, I want to say something to you. Just the two of us. Come on."

She took my arm and pulled me to the side of the room. As we went, I looked up and around for Avril, caught her eye. She was trapped in a conversation with a group of women, grey-haired, in loose linen, ardent.

"There," said Caitlin.

"I'm heading home pretty soon. I'm shattered."

"Not just yet you're not," and she gripped my arm and inspected me with obvious disapproval.

"Actually, you *do* look done in. Well, you'll have to buck up a bit if you're going to be any good as an MP. Now, Selma – *she* had the energy of a dozen people."

"Caitlin, if you're going to have a go at me about Selma again, then can we do it another time? I've got a lot on my mind."

"Have you!" she said,' with some delight. "Ditto."

I had no idea where this was going.

"I said *ditto*."

"I heard you."

She seemed to be rethinking her approach. There was no doubt she wanted to impart something of interest. Funny – I thought it might be some gossip about someone in the room. I hoped it was about the blond man. But it wasn't. She wanted to get something off her chest.

"When I started at *The Messenger*," she told me, "Geoff Mattison gave me three pieces of advice. Follow them, he said, and you'll be a successful editor. Are you listening?"

"Yes, I'm listening."

"The first one was to fall in love with the paper, crass as it sounds. In my eyes, it should be the finest publication in the history of newsprint. The second one was a bit easier. Put the hours in, he said. Like I needed telling. But the third one I didn't see coming. Do you know what it was?"

My mind was so occupied with other things that I could barely focus on what she was saying. I looked around again for Avril, felt I needed her. I saw to my relief that she was coming.

"No," I told her.

"You don't know what his third piece of advice was?"

"No," once again. "I don't."

"He told me to leave you alone."

"I don't follow you."

She laughed at that. Really, she was more elated than I'd ever seen her.

"Wasn't it odd? To be a success at that paper, I had to leave you alone."

"What did he mean?"

"I'll tell you what he meant, he meant that no one should stand in your way. That's all. End of story. But I'm funny like that. It wasn't the end of the story as far as I was concerned. I had to look into it. I had to know why you were untouchable."

"Caitlin, you're talking total bloody rubbish."

She drew back and gave me a withering look.

"Am I?"

"Yes."

She shrugged. "All right then."

I shifted, was impatient. I didn't want to have to understand her. But she wanted me to. The only thing I could do was turn my back on her.

Avril was coming towards us. Her face was a question mark. She was holding her hands up, wanting to know what I was doing. I shook my head, unclear what she asking.

"How funny," I heard Caitlin say. Avril was almost beside me now. "How very, very funny," she went on, raising her voice, finding a new audience member. "All that time writing stories about other people when the story was actually you."

Which was when I felt an almighty and violent force surge past me.

I saw Caitlin, apparently struck by a lightning, struggle and flail, teetering on her ivory white heels for a helpless moment, before falling backwards, wine glass shooting into the air, its contents falling in a quite lovely pale yellow arc as it went.

It was Avril who had shoved her, powerfully with both arms, her hands meeting Caitlin solidly in the chest. I'd seen it but hadn't realised what I was seeing, it happened so quickly.

I heard a scream, many, many gasps, a couple of *what's happeneds* and *oh Gods*.

A shock ran through me. I felt sweat on my forehead and hands.

Avril was standing over Caitlin: two classy, well-dressed professional women, facing off to each other, one of the floor, one standing over her. The conversation in the room was baited.

"Keep your shitty opinions to yourself," I heard Avril say through clenched teeth.

Caitlin took a swipe at one of Avril's feet and Avril stepped back and right into another guest, who dropped his wine and told her to *watch out!*

My old boss was on her knees now, trying to get up. One of her shoes was sitting unoccupied in a space on the floor.

"I know who you are," she said to Avril. "I know who you work for."

Once again Avril lunged towards her, a fist closed and ready.

A man I recognised as a veteran MP and former union fire-brand started forward and grabbed Avril by the top of an arm.

"Come on, love, that's enough."

Avril pulled her arm free, brushed her dress down, sniffed magisterially and swept from the room, with me discreetly following.

One day I'll laugh about it, but I didn't then.

It was an unpleasant thing to witness. Physical violence, people with their blood up, has always unnerved me. I don't like fights. I run away from them.

We walked a little way away from the building in silence. Avril was still giving off small explosions of indignation. I could almost feel them shivering through her body.

"Who?" I asked her, gently. "Avril, who do you work for? Why does Caitlin think it's significant?"

Her face was closed off to me, her mouth shut tight as she tried to control herself.

Finally, she stopped jittering and addressed me.

"I've been working for *you*," she said. "For a long time. And I've had enough. It has to end now."

"I don't know what you mean. You wanted to run my campaign. You seemed so keen. I'm sorry if it's been harder than you thought. I could have told you it would be."

Her look was one of pity and tolerance. She was shaking her head in lieu of finding the right words.

"Do you work for him?" I asked. "The tall fair man that I saw you talking to at the election count? He's some multi-millionaire, you know. Caitlin told me." Still nothing. "Who is he to you?"

Who is he to any of us?

She put a hand on my shoulder but she was steadying herself, not me.

"You take it from here, yeah?"

The afternoon was warm and peaceful. I wandered up to Westminster and perched a moment on the little wall beside the Emmeline Pankhurst monument. It's not a statue I like to look at full-on. Sitting beside it seems so much more friendly and natural.

The traffic careered around Parliament Square and the tourists shuffled along beyond the little fringe of trees that hemmed me in. The Thames sat stock still behind me while the solid world ebbed and flowed around it.

I thought about my parents and my brother and wondered if all I ever wanted was to do better than them and to impress them. Was that at the root of all young decisions: the need to get away from a family? Or indeed, as in the case of my own youngest, a desire to cling on to it. It all starts with a family and spreads out from there.

Why did Danielle want so desperately to excise herself from those who loved her? I had no doubts that they were good and loving people, could hear it in the soft, wounded tones of her big sister.

I had an urge to speak to Willa. It hit me with a jolt that I'd done her a disservice by trying to give her the impression nothing was wrong. Something *was* wrong. Did I really think it would just dissipate? It was late afternoon. Jay would be at his desk unravelling the tortured sentences of one of *The Messenger's* star correspondents. Tess was in the middle of two weeks' work experience at a law firm and Theo was back in college after coming down for the election. Willa would almost certainly be in her college rooms alone. Just the thought of her by herself set my heart beating. It was unbearable.

I fished my phone out of my bag to call her and saw that I had a message.

It was from Kim, Danielle's sister. Why had she messaged me? I'd already forgotten that I'd sent her on a mission.

I opened the message, which contained one word, one set of letters, all mystifying to me until I let the fog clear and understood the extraordinary thing that she was telling me.

Jespersen.

⁂

Moving, moving, slowly, slowly, closer to an understanding. Everyone knows, everyone has an opinion. That's what it felt like. I couldn't stop it. I couldn't get off.

Everyone knows, everyone sees.

But I am always the last. Stupid proud girl, still with her big ideas, and her determination to make something of herself. How slow I am, disastrously slow. I can't see beyond myself. I tell my story as I go along, incapable of standing back and discerning where it will go.

But it's not my story – that's the big joke. If I thought I was telling it, then I was kidding myself. It was being told to me. I should have listened.

I should have known.

3

I STOOD IN front of the house where Danielle had once lived and waited for my nerves to settle.

I'd come out of the Tube at Sloane Square and wandered among the mews and red-brick mansion blocks hoping for a newsagent or café where I could buy a snack so that my hunger wouldn't distract me from the interview ahead. But that just goes to show how little I knew the area. It wasn't the place for corner shops. The only non-residential buildings were small brown churches on corners, orderly and spotless. I wondered if she'd ever attended a service or ever sought a moment's peace inside one of these tasteful little temples.

And so I found myself hungry and edgy at the entrance to a square made up of a fenced-off central garden, towering plane trees and grand white houses on two sides. Huge houses with huge black doors and wide steps leading up to them. They were four neck-craning storeys high with balconies that ran uniformly across the length of all the first-floor windows in the square. Thick pillars stood guard either side of the porches. What struck me was how impenetrable these citadels were, how laughably meagre the pots of white pelargoniums seemed standing before all these massive black doors. And how celestially high. The Jespersen house had no flowers in pots in front of its windows. The place was dark, from the basement behind the cast iron rails to the upper storey windows. A brass door-knocker as big as my hand dominated the top half of the door.

I pressed the bell instead and stepped back.

At eight o'clock the light seemed thin and false. Night was minutes away. The square was utterly silent.

I jumped when something buzzed and clanked behind the door and I heard someone call out: "Just a moment."

The voice was medium-deep, fine-tuned and came with the relaxed fluency of the expensively educated Englishman. Had Avril told him I was coming? It took me nearly an hour of calling to get her to answer and then about the same to prise an address out of her. She told me to leave him alone, that he'd had a bereavement. I told her that his bereavement was one thing, but what about the thirty-year-long suffering of a loving family left in ignorance?

I arrived with nothing to say and no real sense of indignation. What took me there was curiosity. In my mind, he was a Howard Hughes figure, and for all I knew the next few minutes would consist of us awkwardly facing each other on the doorstep before I would have to retire with echoing apologies.

Danielle's husband opened the door and stood in semi-darkness, looking out at me. There was nothing to be read in that face. Avril had implied that she'd be in trouble for letting me disturb him, but this loose assemblage of laid-back humanity didn't strike me as the vindictive type. I couldn't imagine him as an employer, to be honest.

"I wondered if we could talk," I said.

So much taller than me, he seemed to be observing me down the length of his nose.

"Please, do come in," he said, and stepped to one side.

In his dark hallway, Viggo Jespersen and I stood face to

face and immobile. Who had called on whom? I wasn't sure anymore. His next words to me caught me on the hop.

"You hungry?" he asked.

I let out an involuntary guffaw. "You know, I really am."

He led me through the dark, formless space that must have been a hallway or lobby. When we reached a new threshold, he switched on the light and revealed a space of such massive proportions that at first I couldn't conceive of what it was. The floor was tiled in honey-brown stone flags and there were white, wooden cupboards of hospital blandness lining the walls either side of me. At the far end, I saw a counter and two stools, a vast black fridge.

No way! I thought. This is a kitchen. It's actually a kitchen.

We crossed the room and arrived at the fridge.

"Now, let's see what we've got. Many congratulations, by the way, on your election."

"Thank you," I mumbled.

He opened the door and light spilled out. We stood before that sarcophagus of a refrigerator and accustomed our eyes to the glare. Shoulder to shoulder, one as ignorant as the other as to what we might find there, we waited for something.

"Ah," he said and reached in and removed a small bowl of green olives, placing it behind him on the counter. "And this should do."

And this should do was a half wheel of Camembert, wrapped tightly in several layers of cling film and stuck to a saucer. I saw a couple of bottles of tonic water and a carton of almond milk.

No wonder the wealthy seem so emaciated, I thought.

The kitchen lighting was so low that the fridge felt like the only source of comfort and, perversely, heat. We hovered before it, and I was conscious that we were both losing interest in our foraging.

"I'll get some crackers and what have you," he informed me and left my side to rummage through the cupboards.

I turned and sat on one of the bar stools in front of the Camembert and thought how little I fancied it. But he was placing an opened pack of crackers and a cheese knife on the counter and I felt, out of politeness, that I ought to unwrap the many layers and separate a slice from the sagging little block.

"So?" he said, picking through the olives with long, tanned fingers.

I couldn't do anything but smile weakly at him, not knowing what his question meant. Was I supposed to comment on the food?

He rejected the olives and broke apart a cracker.

"What brings you here?"

"I want to ask you about someone," I told him. I couldn't bring myself to say her name.

She was the love of his life.

He smiled at the ragged edge of the cracker.

"Dani?"

I was pulling us closer to her. Would he resist?

"I'm sorry to have called on you at such a time," I said. "But – should you be alone?"

He took a tiny bite of the cracker and kept it somewhere in his cheek.

"Did I say I was alone?"

"No. I just thought because the house was so dark and quiet, that perhaps you were a little . . ."

He was waiting, but I couldn't go on.

"Do you know what I like about having a big house, a *really* big house?" he asked. "I like the fact that it can become my world. There's nothing outside that I need any more or that can't be brought to me, here."

"You've described the life of a very rich hermit."

Viggo Jespersen nodded with a new energy. I'd never come across a human of this sort before. I wasn't even sure he *was* a human. He was built differently (fatless, firm, unyielding) and he sounded different, as though he'd pieced together the language from an instruction manual. Perhaps *homo sapiens* had branched at some distant point in the past and his family came from the other branch.

In short, he was as exotic to me as Danielle Gartner had been.

Could I continue to ask about her now, I wondered? Or should I take his mind off her? I picked up a cracker - noticed with dismay it was one of those expensive thin ones that rattle about in Christmas hampers.

"You knew her."

He said it with resignation, as though putting a marker down.

I gave up on the cracker and said, yes, I'd known her a long time ago, and then only briefly. I'd always wondered what became of her, and that when I heard he was married to her I—

"You what?"

"felt surprised, to be honest, that she was - oh God, how do I say this? - that she had managed to . . ."

"Stay alive for so long?"

I was stumbling, not knowing what would hurt him and what wouldn't.

"She seemed so set on a particular course of action."

He was thoughtful for a while, his fingers dancing on the counter.

"Would you like to see her room?" he asked at last.

"Her room? Yes. Why not?"

We got off our stools and faced each other before he turned on his heels and I followed. Neither of us, it occurred to me for a second, had eaten a thing.

4

"OH MY GOD."
I stood in the doorway and looked at what was,
to all intents and purposes, Danielle's college room from thirty
years ago. A bed, an armchair, and that was it.

There was one difference: we were in the basement, so
there was no window looking down onto parkland, just a
barred skylight trained towards the pavement outside.

"I don't understand," I told him, walking into the centre of
the room, twisting around to inspect every corner.

"What don't you understand?"

"Did she live down here?"

"Well, she slept here."

"But . . . but you were together, right?"

He laughed at that and his eyes widened. They were just
a wide blue expanse.

"Yes, we were together."

"And you slept, here, with her? But why? Your house is a
mansion. Why live down here?"

He fell into the armchair. His long legs rucked up at once
and his hands dangled between them. He couldn't have looked
more out of place.

"No, I didn't sleep down here. I have more of a . . . taste
for luxury. Not just a taste – a need."

I backed towards the bed, my eyes still on him, and sat
down. The bed was pushed up against a wall. I shuffled in
retreat until my back was against it.

"May I ask you a question about her?"

"Go ahead."

"How did you meet her?"

"Ah." Thank God there was a smile. When he spoke, he didn't seem sentimental so much as entertained.

"We were both university drop-outs," he told me.

"I knew *she* was."

"Well, so was I. Though from a different university. We were in a residential care home when we came across each other. Both of us very young, both put there by parents struggling to understand us. I think hers were deeply devoted to her and her health. Mine were merely feeling helpless and not a little embarrassed."

"What kind of care home?"

"Oh, one of those thorough monastic places. They were all the rage at the time. Young people with all manner of problems lumped together and told to get it all out of their systems. My father could easily afford it. Hers, not so much. She'd literally left university and gone straight there. Funny thing."

So, only days after I met her. Danielle's parents must have picked her up and booked her into this clinic straight away. Maybe they used their life savings to do it.

"And you fell in love?"

I thought the reminder of romance might please him. Or madden him with grief. Neither seemed to be the case. Each time he dropped his head and inspected his feet, I saw something new, the little wings of white at his temples, the spare frame of his chest and shoulders, the elegant bow of his long arms.

"We became inseparable, as a matter of fact."

I could see it – the rightness of these two beautiful young people running into each other at their most desperate moment.

"I'm so glad," I told him. "How very lucky she was to have found you."

"We were both fortunate."

"And you married?"

"We did."

"I never forgot her," I said, quickly. "I never could get her out of my mind. She convinced me that she wouldn't last long, that she wanted to escape the world. I really felt sure she would do it. But she fell in love instead. I wish I'd made more of an effort to find out what happened to her. Maybe even kept in touch. I just felt so certain that she wouldn't want me to. We said goodbye."

"What can I tell you? We had a good life here, just the two of us. Nobody bothered us and we lived in exactly the way we wanted."

"That's nice," I told him. "Did she not go out to work?"

"Neither of us worked."

"Oh."

"We watched a lot of films."

For thirty years! You watched films for thirty years?

"We were lucky," he went on. "I could call on family wealth. My father is pretty lavish with his money when it comes to his children. The company makes money hand over fist and my father's children can have as much of it as they want as long as they are God-fearing, respectable and straight."

I waited a moment, then let myself laugh a little and he waited another moment before joining in.

"And you don't work for the company?"

"Well, he's still alive and still runs it, but I'm allowed to make the odd little decision, a donation here, an appointment there. Just enough to give the impression that I'm a trusted scion."

"Is it even a company?" I asked. "I don't really know."

"Oh, here we go! The spiel. We're what you call a conglomerate. Several stand-alone businesses in diverse fields stuck together under our ownership. And many strategic partnerships and investments. My grandfather was in shipping in Sweden. My father took us into IT and Media. I was born here while he was doing that."

"Too many questions. Sorry."

He held up his hands.

"A good thing for an MP, I'd have thought."

Oh God, I was an MP. I'd managed to forget. How low I felt at the thought of it. My phone buzzed in my pocket. I'd turned off the ringer but the noise was audible. I apologised and ignored it.

"I like your Christian name," I told him.

I could picture her mouth saying it.

"So do I! Best thing the old man did for me."

And so we sat, me on the bed, him in the chair, and we chatted a little about the house and about the two maids who came every day to clean it and to cook for him. He told me how he wasn't keen on the area but knew the minute he saw the building that it would be right for them. I asked about the number of rooms, tried to pry gently into whether they'd had children, but knew they hadn't. No parent my age would leave such details unsaid.

What an attractive couple they must have been. Kindred spirits. What an appalling shame that it ended and he was alone. He didn't strike me as lost or vulnerable, just incomplete, in need of a new companion. No one would match up to her.

"You're very welcome to look around, but I doubt you came for that."

"What did I come for?" I asked him, slightly dreamily.

"To find out if she killed herself."

I wriggled forward on the bed as though I might have to run at any moment.

"Did she?" I asked.

"We were the best thing that could have happened to each other. You should know that. But it was chance that brought us together. She never planned it that way."

"Of course not. No one ever plans love. Are you saying she would have ended things, had she not met you?"

"I don't know. Probably. I wasn't what she planned. I just became part of the plan."

"I don't really understand you."

And then he got up. That was all I was getting.

I felt a rush of anxiety. I didn't want to leave him or his house. I didn't want to go back to the world and my responsibilities. I didn't want to care about my husband and my children and I most definitely did not want to serve a constituency or to listen to endless complaints from people I neither knew nor respected. I could stay here! I could stay with Viggo Jespersen or in Danielle's room. I'd be happy alone. I could live on his meagre diet.

I was losing my mind.

My brain was ticking over fast, trying to find ways of pleasing him. I felt strongly that I wanted to please him. But I knew that my time with him was running out. He looked at the dark staircase and then back at me.

"I have things to do, I'm afraid. I hate to be rude. I just have some business to get sorted. And, well the thing is, I do prefer to be alone."

He left the basement room and started climbing the steps to the ground floor. I watched his back dumbly as he ascended. What was happening?

"Wait," I called.

I went to the foot of the steps.

"What kind of life did you have together? Don't tell me you watched movies all day."

"That's exactly what we did," he called back.

I paused, one foot on the bottom step, lingering in Danielle's world, peering up into Viggo's, as she must have done.

"She was so extraordinary," I told him. "Her mind was exceptional. I don't believe she simply let it all . . . go to waste."

He was at the top of the stairs, by the front door. I ran up and found to my dismay that he already had the handle in his grasp.

"She had her projects," he said, with the same spare, haunted look in his eyes I'd first seen at the election count. He opened the front door. It was dark outside and the street lamps were lit. I saw the fenced-off communal garden beyond the door. Did anyone ever use it? I couldn't imagine any children playing there. There was no one about, but I could hear distant traffic. An early summer night in a sleepless city.

Viggo's manner had changed. He felt younger to me now, as reluctant as I was to take the lead on anything, as keen to retire.

A breeze from the dark core of the square brought with it a faint smell of honeysuckle.

I stepped across the threshold, and as I put myself outside the Gartner-Jespersen stronghold, felt the urge to run straight back in. He was about to close the door.

"So, you said it was cancer, just for appearances?"

Only his face and right shoulder were now visible.

"It was a family requirement by the Jespersens. We'd planned it that way."

"What have you told her family?"

"Only that she's dead."

It came as a blow, his tolling words.

"That's hardly fair to them," I said with growing emotion. "Can't you see how terrible it must be for them, to be told out of the blue like this. It's heartless."

"I'm sure you'll fill them in." And then he added, almost reprimanding himself: "It never occurred to me that you might be in touch with them. But, of course. That's why you're here."

He wanted me out of the house. But why push me out so soon? Was it that he couldn't trust himself?

"I don't understand," I pleaded. "She'd been all right for so long. For years. She had *you* and this amazing house, and money. She had love, Viggo. Why did she give up now?"

I felt his glare pushing me out and down the road. I stepped backwards, away from it. The door was closing, his face receding.

"Because her project was over. Goodnight."

The door was shut, and I was alone.

5

You HAVE TO run out and meet the world and embrace it, my aunt Deirdra said.

Because people are good. People are born good and crave goodness from others. Don't believe what they say about complicated souls, she told me. Don't believe this rubbish about an inner fight.

We are good!

The years add layers and with each year and each layer you wonder at how ignorant you were the year before. I know more now than I ever did before, you tell yourself. I'll never be as clever about things as I am now. But of course the next year comes, and the next layer, and you think back and you shudder at your idiocy. When will I know the truth? At the end?

I never loved the world as Deirdra wanted me to.

None of it ever convinced me because it was all just words. The words of children. Or *childish* words. *Good. Bad.* Right and wrong. Everyone else seemed to believe in the simplicity of their truth. Why couldn't I? Maybe because Danielle had never let me.

༺

On either side of me, tall houses, white, like cliffs outlined against the night sky. Enormous silent places, not homes, but exquisite refuges, hermetic. You close a door and you seal yourself in. Wealth buys you this: removal. And when you are this removed, the world outside can be anything you want it to be. It might as well be a dream. Or a game. For you, nothing need move on. You can spend an entire day, and even a night, mulling over words spoken years before. You can work on your favourite puzzle: meanings.

What does it mean to be good?

﹏

I reached up to my face and brought down a tear on the tip of my finger and gazed at it.

Why was I crying?

I placed the tear on the blunt spike of a cast iron railing. It still seemed so bizarre to me, this signifier of my misery. I had no idea that tears were coming. I was not aware of being miserable.

I was standing on the broad front step, hadn't moved since he threw me out. Before me was that great black door. To my right were the iron railings and below them the basement area. A small window.

I reached for the doorbell. I wouldn't look, but I was sure there was a young woman staring up at me from that window, defiant. *You're not coming in. Don't let her in!*

I pressed the button, over and over. The sound echoed around the square, loud as a siren.

Day after day she looked idly through that window, barely caring about the feet that passed by, or the neighbours, or the neighbourhood. All she needed was there, within her. People gave her things, tokens of love and friendship, but she never wanted them. Never saw the attraction in the material. A dress

234

was a dress, given to her once by her mother, worn because it felt cool against her skin on an unbearably hot day. How she looked in it was of no interest to her.

The inanimate had no meaning. And meaning was all that she desired.

I felt a tear run down and into my open mouth. The project was over.

6

"THE BIGGEST SURPRISE when we met was that we were so similar. Roughly the same age, both young and attractive, very clever people – if you don't mind my saying so. And both of us intent on doing away with ourselves. It made us laugh, to tell you the truth. Oh, and we'd both reached a turning point."

I was sitting in his living room, a couple of wall lights providing the faintest glow, the brandy glass in my hands reflecting it back weakly into my eyes. He was in an armchair opposite mine. The strange distribution of light meant that I barely saw him. His steady, fascinating voice reached me from somewhere I couldn't fathom.

"It was my father, you see. He was very attentive and generous, but a total bastard. Sorry, I ought to clarify: he still is a total bastard. He still controls me and my siblings and the family brand. We are the company and the company is us. And we come from a family of revolting religious zealots. When we were teenagers, he'd say: 'All I ask is that you don't embarrass us or damage our good name back home.' And he knew – my mother certainly did – about my leanings, and there was no question that I would ever be able to live publicly the way nature intended me to. Or not if I wanted to remain wealthy."

I took a sip from my glass and the numbing effect was almost instant. I closed my eyes and forced myself to concentrate on him and to hear him.

"I developed into a ruined kind of person. Does that make sense? By the time I was twenty, it was over for me. I wanted to be detached from everyone and everything. Rotten kind of life for such a young man. I was angry and resentful, but powerless with it. Because I so wanted the money. I had to be able to lead a life of total detachment and in a space big enough for it not to matter. I'd show him. I'd either kill myself or I'd take the money and live on my own terms. And that's when I met her."

His voice faltered and I thought I heard some repressed emotion for the first time. But then he must have been a master of repression. An expert in leading an approximated life. My eyes sought his in the gloom, but he wasn't in the mood for being looked at.

"And what was *her* turning point?" I asked.

"You were."

Ten minutes earlier, he'd opened the door to me, stood wordlessly as I walked past him and broke the seal once more. He'd seemed as coldly surprised by my damp eyes as I had been. I think they scared him. It must have become clear to him, then, that I wouldn't leave until I knew.

"I don't understand how."

"We talked about goodness, you see. We sat in that wretched home, with its ghastly rose-pink walls and its obnoxiously caring staff, and we discussed the meaning of goodness and she said she'd been thinking about it from the moment she met you. She talked about the night you were sent to keep watch over her – how you'd been so excitedly ambitious, and how, rather than resenting you for it, she became . . . attached to an idea. You see, up to that point she'd only felt that she was a freak and that there was no biological reason for her to be alive."

Once more I didn't grasp what was being said and told him so.

He gave the mildest of shrugs. A signal that he could easily end up being bored by all of this. But he went on all the same.

"She had an operation when she was sixteen, a rare procedure for a teenage girl, but apparently her life had depended on it. They had to remove a tumour and took the ovaries with it. She felt things a little *deeply* at the best of times. But this one, she couldn't get over. She convinced herself that there was simply no point to her, no future. She said she'd never experience the emergence of new life from her body. To say she was depressed by this would not be quite accurate. She could have got over depression or been helped to get over it. No, she simply ceased to believe in herself as a viable human being. Ending herself had a neatness and logic to it."

Viggo stopped and I heard him sip from his own drink.

"I never knew any of this," I murmured.

"Of course you didn't. It was none of your business."

"But I had this feeling she needed looking after."

I saw a dim smile above the brandy glass.

"Did you? I can't imagine she asked you to. Would've hated it, if I knew her right. She'd been rather blunt with her parents one day, telling them that she couldn't bear to remain alive, and their collapse frightened her."

"Those poor people." I shuddered. But he returned another of those neutral shrugs. "And anyway, it didn't stop her."

"It did and it didn't. It made her waver. But you – you sparked something new in her heart. You may have felt that you were mothering *her* when you kept watch that night, but no. She listened to you telling her how you would change the world and she felt nothing should stop you doing it. Nothing should get in your way. Everything should support you in your dream. She wanted to place two loving and protecting arms round your life, as it were. If she wasn't allowed the neat end, then she would have to re-think herself."

The more he talked about her, the further she receded. To hear her described, her thoughts captured, her ideas explained, was to look at a stranger.

Viggo turned his head to the side and his features were lost to the darkness.

"Selflessness, she told me, was not about achieving things for the benefit of others. It wasn't about *others* at all. It was about emptying yourself of any feeling and desire, so that someone else might make practical use of you. Giving a life you couldn't use in the first place. That nullifying sacrifice appealed to me, too, at the time."

She was slipping even further from me now. I wanted to stop him and to go over what he was saying, but I kept quiet, kept my eye on that dress as it disappeared around every corner.

"And so we made a decision, sitting there in that room, with that dreadful food and people festering around the place. We would get married. Why not? I would get a beautiful wife and my family's approval along with a private income and a house of choice wherever I wanted it. Houses plural, if I preferred. She would get to use that income and influence in any way she pleased. We would be together and yet alone. And no one need know what our lives were like. Who cared, anyway? As long as both sets of parents thought we were settled and happy.

"We became reclusive – we only ventured out when we really had to. I went out more than her. She hardly set foot outside the door. Occasionally we had no choice but to emerge as a couple and then we ran from any attention and anyway I was able to limit the press interest."

Viggo paused – was forming some words, rejecting others – but I couldn't wait.

"Just say it. Tell me what you did."

He seemed surprised by my spirit.

"We got you your dream. We helped you along the way. We did something selfless – by creating a useful person. If you like – if it makes better sense to you – by creating a *good* person."

"How?" I demanded. "I did it all, not you."

"Well . . ."

"I got my jobs, I did it all."

I was shaking my head, refusing to understand.

"The *Messenger*, the job on the *Messenger*," I insisted.

"My family's company has a stake in the *Messenger*. Normally a silent partner makes no executive decisions in a company. But we were behind the paper's digital rebirth and my interference was, let's say, tolerated. I asked them to create the trainee post. Dani spoke indirectly to a relative of yours. An aunt, was it? She rather enjoyed all that."

"No. Sorry, no. It doesn't work like that."

"That's exactly how it works. You'd done all the leg work, got yourself trained, with a little financial help from us. She made sure the right door was open to you. I just had a quiet word now and again, to put things on the right track."

"To make sure I wasn't sacked for being shit! To make sure I was promoted above more competent colleagues."

"Now, now."

"Don't fucking *now now* me."

As with the tears, I hadn't sensed the anger coming. He could see it all of course. He watched my face intently now, anticipating every moment of dawning that played across it.

"That news story . . ." I whispered. "It turned my career around."

"Yew Lodge. Terrible place."

"That's where you both met. I've been there!"

"Her parents didn't know what it was like. Thought they were protecting her. My parents knew perfectly well. You spoke to Aaron French, of course. You remember what he was like. Utterly broken. Could never forgive his father for it. I told him one day we'd get our own back."

"And you used me?"

"Aaron was a dear, dear, beautiful boy. You exposed the place and stopped others from going through what he and I did. It's normal, surely, for a journalist to be tipped off about things by unhappy people?"

There isn't time to assess a life in a few seconds. It takes a life to know a life. I couldn't sit there and flit from moment to moment, weighing each one up and asking myself which was fraudulent, and which not.

"Anything? Did I do anything myself?"

He didn't appear concerned, just curious about the effect his words were having. I knew what he was doing. He was giving me enough time to work it out.

"Avril!" I cried out.

"*There's* a wonderful woman," he reflected. "You want to know what good is? Go no further."

"How long?"

"From the start."

And now Avril's face was before me. I saw a young woman,

eager to take up any opportunity, accepting the help of benefactors, understanding how the world worked, grateful for what she got.

"She liked you so much. Felt indebted to you. I was very discreet. I paid her way through university and training, got her her first job, and eventually she worked for me. She didn't know the details or my motivation. She just knew that part of the deal was that you were to be looked after."

"In return, she got a fortune."

"No," he said firmly. "In return, she got a chance to make something of her life and to make use of her considerable gifts. She's wonderfully down-to-earth. And, by the by, she truly wanted the best for you as well. Felt that she and you had the same spirit and drive. I'm not sure she was right about that."

I was listening to my life. *Listening* to it. How could this stranger know me? All the facts were familiar to him and yet seemed to be presenting themselves as new to me.

"Avril persuaded me to stand," I said. "She seemed so excited. But she was just doing as she was told, as *you* told her. Selma! You ruined a perfectly good woman's career to get me her seat."

"You don't understand."

"That poor woman."

"That poor woman," he said, pressing his glass against his cheek, "will be fine, has accepted a little help with buying a holiday home abroad. From what I heard, she was an excellent MP, but that husband of hers . . ."

"How did you know?" I asked and heard the scorn in my voice. "You're not trying to tell me that you and Danielle turned detective? That you went investigating and dug up the dirt?"

"Good God, no. I've never set foot in your neck of the woods and don't intend to. No, that was Avril. She was my little fixer. Kept an eye on you."

And now a rising panic. A softening, a sick feeling, the feeling you have when someone close to you dies. A feeling of finality from which you can't escape. I was the one dying. Didn't he see this disintegration coming? What did he think I would do? Get up and shake him by the hand?

"Will I be the first? What will they say? Will they even allow it?"

He got up from his chair and looked down at me. For the first time, he seemed worried.

"What are you talking about? I think we should bring this conversation to an end now."

"If I resign straight away. Will they let me? A by-election right after an election. We could say I was ill. My children – will it ruin their futures? I'll have a reputation."

I was gabbling and he was open-mouthed.

"What will they say? Our friends . . . the voters . . ."

"I'm going to call you a car to take you home. Wait there."

"No!"

The phone was buzzing in my pocket again.

I wouldn't let him go.

"You've got to sort this out. Put everything right. I'm going to resign. I'm a fraud. All of this is fraudulent."

"Don't be ridiculous."

The buzzing phone. The rising panic. How had he not foreseen this?

"Listen," he said. "It's not easy being elected to Parliament. You couldn't have done it if you didn't have it in you. My donations opened doors, and it was vital you didn't stain yourself with our money. But people voted for you because they believed in you. We simply kept things on track."

"On track! You directed my life the way you thought it should go."

"The way you felt so passionately it should go."

"But I was a *child*. A child, when I told her. My life could have gone in any direction. It didn't need someone pulling strings. I was her game."

"You were not her game. You were her cause."

"She had no right."

Viggo's expression hardened.

"You have no idea," he reflected bitterly. "The years and years of waiting. The emptiness. The waking up day after day with nothing but the tiniest hope that she might be of use to someone, that she might create something of value. I'm glad for her. I envy her, if you must know. I'm calling you a car."

He left the room and I got up, alarmed, not wanting to be alone. I would have followed him, kept on at him for more, for some kind of relief, but the phone – it wouldn't stop.

I took it out of my pocket, but I couldn't look at the screen. Too many questions, images passing back and forth, distraction. A whirlwind. How could I concentrate enough to answer a phone? By now I could only think of one thing. One name. A name beyond dear to me.

Was he ever mine? Was any of it real?

7

"ARE N'T YOU GOING to answer it?" Viggo asked. He had returned to the living room and now had his back to me as he made himself a drink. He was leaning over a sideboard, his fingers hopping across a series of bottles, landing on one and removing its stopper. There was something light about his actions. Or lightened. He wasn't the same man. He'd said everything and now it was time for me to go and leave him alone in his house. I watched his back – his pale blue shirt vivid in the shadows – and tried to calm my voice before speaking.

"I need to know if you sent him to me."

He turned. "Who?" he said, airily.

"My husband. Jay Corey. The man I fell in love with. Who appeared at exactly the right moment, saved me from a relationship that . . ." As the words left my mouth, their significance became clear. "Simon," I said.

"You had such a lovely little flat, by all accounts. Can I offer you another drink? I'm not used to being hospitable, forgive me."

"He just went away," I said, desolately.

Viggo fixed me with a stare that I tried so hard to deflect but couldn't. It was asking: *do you really want to know?*

"Yes," he said. "He went away. And you're right, he would never have let you thrive. He would have curtailed your dreams, your freedom. We dealt with it. That's the past. Let it go."

I wasn't allowed to interject.

"Night after night, we discussed you and your bloody love life. She felt so strongly that she knew who would be right for you. I had to report back to her on all the potential candidates. Never saw her so animated as when we went through the possibilities."

I must have swayed because he stepped forward.

"I feel a bit odd," I told him.

He looked deeply dismayed.

"You're not going to throw up, are you? The car will be here any minute."

I sat back down on the armchair and closed my eyes.

"I love him," I said. I had to concentrate on keeping the sick feeling down. "We found each other. We genuinely fell in love."

"Oh, you did, you did," said Viggo, though the concern I heard in his voice was probably for his carpet. "She saw it coming, got it bang on, my clever girl. Timed it all so perfectly. But we had others on the list, if that one didn't work out."

"No. We found each other."

"Yes, yes. You found each other. If that's what you want me to say."

I had to steady myself, control my nerves, keep the hysteria at bay. Eyes still closed. A moment of stillness. We were both on the brink. I couldn't let myself be overwhelmed. I opened my eyes and I saw Viggo, back in the opposite armchair, his expression sombre.

"You're right," he said. "Even the most skilled matchmaker in the world couldn't make two people actually fall in love.

They might see the potential. They might even make the circumstances right, but there's only one way that it works, and that's if you're truly right for each other. *He* had no idea, no idea at all.

"I never let myself have what you had," he added and looked away in case I caught what was there, in those vaporous blue eyes. "You're one of the lucky ones."

Should I cry for Viggo? For a young man so injured by his family that he'd signed up to an insane plan at his most vulnerable moment? It left him with nothing but this . . . this mausoleum of a house. Had anyone ever sat with him in this room and listened?

It was such an unhomely place, the furniture solid and heavy, wood-framed armchairs that would have seated two people quite comfortably. There were several paintings, the largest a rural scene, woodland, Scandinavian-looking. It was framed heavily in gold and was so broad that no ordinary house would have had enough wall space for it. There were no signs of normal comings-and-goings, of anything left carelessly behind. No traces of family. Nothing sentimental or trivial.

I couldn't help it, my thoughts turned to that small, characterless basement room, and to the two of them, him in the chair, her on the bed, talking late into the night – the distinction between night and day possibly not even featuring in their lives. He would report back what he'd seen: the young woman going for an interview on *The Messenger*, passing her in the corridor. What would he have told Danielle? What I wore? What my expression was?

And what did she feel? Triumph? That she was holding me in the palm of her hand?

Or that she was a step closer to her release?

"Why didn't she ever approach me?" I asked him. "Didn't she want to?"

Viggo was still distant from his musings about love. He had to pull himself back to me.

"Oh, she did, she did. She wanted to so much. And then, finally, she allowed herself to be with you. Just once. To say goodbye."

I shook my head.

"What? She was never with me. You've got that wrong."

"You were asleep."

"No. Sorry. That's wrong."

"She kissed your hand and left."

A denial was in the process of forming again when all at once I felt the skin on the back of my hand shiver, as though a kiss had just been planted on it. It took me back to just a few days ago. The memory of a sensation when I hadn't even been conscious. In the cinema.

She had sat beside me in the cinema.

"And there were times when she needed to be close to you but daren't give herself away . . ."

"My bed. She slept overnight in my empty flat."

A nod of approval. He might as well have been scoring me.

"We bought the letting company to give us access."

"Huh."

It was a laugh, but it came out in a bitter little pop.

The excessive darkness in this vast room was strange and disorientating. Lights had been placed strategically to pick out rare treasures. Only now did I notice an art deco statue of a deer, on a stand in a far corner, lit up from below. I could envisage him here at night, when he'd left her, looking from one acquisition to another, barely able to see the back of his hand.

"Please," Viggo said. "Just answer your phone. It's becoming irritating."

It was buzzing in my hand, had been doing so on and off for who knows how long. I nursed it in my palm, hoping it would finally give out and die. I nodded. He was right. I had to let the rest of my world in. As soon as I pressed the button and held it to my ear, Jay was there.

"Where the hell have you been? Why didn't you answer?"

"Sorry," I said. "I'm sorry. I've been busy. I'm coming home now."

"It's Willa," and his voice broke.

I had to shake my brain to attention.

"What is it?"

"They've called from the college. She told a friend that she can't go on. They discovered a stash of pills."

"Oh Jay. No."

"I told you! I told you she couldn't cope alone. We should be there with her. She's our daughter."

"We should. We have to be with her."

"Where have you been?"

I got to my feet. Viggo was sitting up and alert in his chair, watching me.

"Yes, we've got to go. Now. I'll be at Sloane Square Tube, waiting. Pick me up from there."

From the phone in my fist I heard my husband's distant voice.

"Where have you been?"

"Please. Just come for me."

"I have to go," I told Viggo. "There's an emergency. My daughter."

"The car should be here."

249

"I don't want your fucking car."

He got up and I heard him leave the house and run down the steps, while a new image formed in my mind. A girl on her bed in her university room, convinced nobody was coming.

⚜

He was blocking my way, stopping me from leaving the house.

"I'm not sure you're strong enough. You look very pale. Just wait one moment and the car will be here."

"I need to go," I said and, as I said it, I saw over his shoulder a black car pull up in front of the house.

He was evidently relieved.

"It's here. Go. I hope everything works out –"

"Don't," I said. "Don't hope anything for me. Don't think about me, don't come near me. We will never see each other again."

He held up his hands in submission.

I walked past him and arrived on the stone steps, the slightest of warm breezes cooling my face and calming my heartbeat. The square was, of course, silent and secretive, but the city still audible beyond it.

I was about to go down the steps when I stopped and turned back to him. Even with that picture of Willa in my mind, another thought was coming. A question was pressing to be asked.

"Why did you tell me everything?" I said. "She must have wanted it all to go to the grave with her. You've spoilt her whole notion of the ultimate selfless act."

The engine of the waiting car rumbled. I caught the sound of the radio inside.

"I thought you might ask me that."

"I think I know," I said, hurriedly. "It was Caitlin, wasn't it? My boss on *The Messenger*. She was intrigued and sniffing around and had worked things out. She was going to expose you or confront you or something."

He shook his head.

"No, she has no control over me. She knows not to go too far. I wouldn't have insisted on her appointment if I'd thought she'd work it out or cause any trouble. Her husband, Hugh, is an old schoolfriend of mine. She just needed a job."

"Then why? *Why* did you tell me?"

Viggo Jespersen seemed diminished for the first time. He had come down to earth at last. I wondered if he'd ever hated it or felt sullied by it, having to remove himself from his sanctuary to go out into the world, to dirty his hands with all her crazy commands. Had he at any point regretted any of it? And would he miss it, now that it was over?

I pushed him again: "Please tell me why?"

He looked anxiously at the car.

"Your daughter," he said.

"Why?" I insisted.

"Because I saw you in that room among all those ambitious, pushy, self-promoting people, and you looked like a truck had hit you. It was like I saw you for the first time. That's why I finally let Avril send you. There's still time you see, to live a true life."

"Time for me?" I asked.

"Yes," he said, then added rather wistfully: "And for me perhaps."

It was finished. Everything was finished. The project. The act of pure goodness. The ultimate selflessness. The idea born on a stifling summer's night in a student room. Two girls had created it, one unwittingly, the other enjoying a strange sense of purpose at last.

A girl had died. That was all. A girl, who had put off her death, was now dead.

You were so beautiful. But you were never loved, never touched, never seen.

How could you have thought that I would be enough for you?

I walked past the white pillars that guarded the entrance and heard the door close behind me. At the same time, the car door opened.

"No, thank you," I told the driver. "I'll make my own way."

THE END

EPILOGUE

I'VE BEEN TELLING her stories. I snatch at memories like they're flakes of ash circling my head, some of them darting from my grasp, some landing in my palm, only to disintegrate. But there are enough of them to keep me talking, if only quietly and disjointedly.

She is sleeping, her head in my lap, both of us on her bed. When she was very young, she would fall asleep to my voice and wake up as soon as I stopped talking. I took to phoning relatives in the evening, with my daughter in my arms, making call after call, getting them over with, lulling her at the same time. I'd stroke the length of her nose with the tip of my finger, delicately, the signal for her to close her eyes. She doesn't hear what I'm saying, only knows somewhere in her subconscious that I'm talking.

When we arrived, Willa held out her arms to me and crawled on to me, and that, it seemed, was the signal for Jay to leave. Wordlessly. We didn't even notice he'd gone.

In the car, heading north, we'd said very little. The night was the unfurling of a road beneath headlamps. A silent journey, two overwrought travelling companions, too tense to produce words. I didn't have any. He was angry, or sad, or something else he couldn't communicate.

We arrived with the light to the sight of a curled-up girl, her tutor sitting beside her, bleary-eyed, grateful for the relief.

"We've not really spoken," said the woman. "I thought she ought to rest."

Within moments, the tutor had gone, so had Jay, and Willa and I were together.

The day is filling with sound. Through the open window I can hear the voices of young people. We are in a ground floor room in a small Victorian house in a narrow city street. There is life all around us, young people coming and going, heading to lectures and tutorials, I presume. These houses are nearly all student accommodation, ragged and characterful, one with a political banner hung across the window so everyone can see how earnest and angry the residents are.

I hear a group of girls laughing as they pass by the window. They are talking about a boy and about the night before. Their voices swoop and loop about like ecstatic birds. One of them is joyfully scandalised. *You did what with him?*

Then the front door slams and Jay arrives back in the room carrying a bulging plastic bag and two coffees. He is still in yesterday's work shirt, the sleeves – naturally – rolled up.

I can see in his face that he has struggled. Nothing passes through his mind without it leaving a trace. He has so many smiles. I know them all. What they mean. What they hide.

"I've brought us some breakfast," he says.

He starts to unpack, putting the items not on the bed or the desk but on a flattened-out bag on the floor. He has bought croissants – large, fresh, golden-brown – a jar of apricot jam, a tub of butter, some apples, bananas and yoghurt. He also has three chocolate bars – our various favourites.

"Well," I say, gently pushing Willa's head off my lap and joining him on the floor. "At least she's not an anorexic."

A genuine, spontaneous laugh from him now.

"A floor picnic," he says. "Willa's finest invention."

He removes a packet of plastic cutlery – one setting – from his pocket and holds it up proudly.

"Bloody hero," I say.

I watch his hands as he opens the jam jar and lays the lid carefully on our picnic blanket. He offers me the jar and, as I take it, I should be calm, I should be content, but my heart is speeding and my throat constricting. I won't cry. I *won't*. But how can I not?

When he finishes his croissant, he looks away and I can enjoy my favourite view of him, his profile, crinkles at the eyes, greying furze from head to chin. Crumbs in the furze.

"It's like always starting again. With Willa, I mean. Having to work it out."

"Hasn't it always been like that with all of them?" he asks.

His eyes seem suddenly to light up and I follow his gaze and see that Willa (possibly hearing her name) is waking.

"Give me that Bounty right now," she says.

We pack her room together, the three of us, mainly the two of us, Willa dawdling over every task. When we leave the house, a passing girl calls Willa over and the two of them start an animated conversation on the pavement, while Jay and I pack the car.

I stop for a moment and watch them. They look to me like any other pair of nineteen-year-olds, on the cusp, near-women. Their language is one of crisis and catastrophe made everyday.

I hear Jay grunt as he shoves a cardboard box full of bedding into the boot.

"She'll be all right," he says to himself.

We drive home. Four hours, no stopping and when we see London – the spiked, stacked, serrated mass of it – I put a hand on Jay's thigh and he places his hand on mine. It's like always having to start again.

ACKNOWLEDGMENTS

"**N**OBODY EVER WRITES a book alone," you said, Kate. You were absolutely right. I am deeply indebted to you and to Jen, Mark, Rosalind, Rob and Will.